CONTENTS UNDER PRESSURE

Collected Stories

Ellen Prentiss Campbell

for Eleanor, with me from the beginning

Table of Contents

Depth Perception   7

Sea Change   21

Peripheral Vision   37

Entangled Objects   51

Chinese Vermilion   65

Shade Gardening   81

The Bicycle Lesson   95

White Laurel   109

Idlewild   129

Dance Lessons   147

Artesian Springs   159

About the Author   173

Depth Perception

Lily finally did the pregnancy test one afternoon, in their windowless bathroom. Lam was out, teaching. Afterward, in the kitchen, she put beef bones to simmer for *pho ba* — her only Vietnamese dish, learnt in an Extension School cooking class. Losing herself in the anodyne of chopping ginger, cilantro, basil, and scallions with a razor sharp knife, she absorbed the test result. She would tell him over dinner; he would put down his bowl, his chopsticks. He would listen.

But they ate the soup accompanied by the news on the radio. She made no announcement. She washed the dishes; they studied. She went to bed alone.

Lily watched the minutes change on the clock radio until at midnight she shoved back the covers and walked to the living room. Lam hunched over the computer keyboard, playing solitaire, pale in the flickering underwater light of the monitor.

"Come to bed."

"Soon," he said without looking up. "I'm relaxing." His sharp shoulders jutted out beneath the two layers of sweaters he wore to stay warm in the drafty apartment.

"I could help with that."

"Later. If you're still up."

Almost Thanksgiving, and he would defend his dissertation on attachment theory the second week in December. He prepared with an athlete's intensity; she envied his concentration and stamina. Once, Lily had been a night owl too. Their circadian rhythms had meshed: they ran before dinner, through the neighborhood, up to the lake, around the Midway, showered together, prepared their meal, and ate it kneeling at the low table beside the bay window. Every evening they had studied side by side, fueled by a carafe of green tea. After the last drop of the last cup they slipped into bed, often rallying and making love before drifting asleep.

But now they inhabited different time zones although both were graduate students at the University of Chicago. He never left

Hyde Park while three days a week she journeyed downtown to the final field placement of her social work program. Evenings, after the bus ride and walk home, she felt as though someone had pulled a plug and all her energy had leaked away. He ran; she napped. After dinner Lily cut and pasted her thesis draft, until fatigue defeated her. Lam labored on, his industry a silent reproach. He came to bed long after she fell asleep.

Lily preferred her internship days at the adoption agency to the campus and the classroom. Her supervisor praised her work, and how quickly Lily learned to speak the language of adoption — to say relinquishment rather than giving up; dissolution, not giving back. To speak of permanence. Lily herself was adopted from Vietnam, thirty years earlier, by way of Catholic Charities in Baltimore.

The supervisor hinted at a job offer. Though Lily had originally intended to do adoption work, now she wasn't sure. On home visits she felt like a voyeur; she struggled over her case summaries and recommendations — uneasy with her power over lives, uncomfortable passing judgment. And in spite of the responsibility, the money wasn't good — even for social work. The agency only paid by the case, upon each completed placement.

"It seems like a conflict of interest, like an incentive to approve families," she worried to Lam.

"You're in the business of brokering babies," he shrugged, cutting off discussion. He was impatient with her recently. She hoped it would improve once he defended his dissertation.

In the coffee lounge at the agency a newspaper clipping on the bulletin board showed an American man, late-middle-aged, with his arm around a young Eurasian woman, smiling above the caption: *Veterans Group Reunites Viet Children of GIs with their Fathers.* A retired American intelligence officer, he had made it his mission to reunite veterans with children they'd fathered during the war. He'd built a database, a website. With her round Caucasian eyes and long nose, Lily had always assumed she was an American soldier's unknown, left-behind souvenir.

She copied the article and showed Lam. "Maybe he could find my birth father, if I knew his name."

"Leave it alone, Lily." He used to call her Hue, Vietnamese for the flower.

"I want to know who I am."

"Lily Kirk, from Evanston. You were born, you got out. You're lucky."

He made her feel guilty for her comfortable life — adopted at seven months into a middle-class world. But hadn't she come into that life by losing everything, too, even if she hadn't escaped in a boat and come ashore in an uncle's overcrowded household outside Pittsburgh?

Lily grew up with the bedtime story of how she became her parents' chosen child: rescued from Saigon as it fell, brought by the Sisters of the Sacred Heart Orphanage to the last baby-lift plane out on April 26, 1974. The incomplete fairy tale made no mention of her birth parents. Lily had shied away from asking, though she wondered — especially after her high school class visited Washington, D.C.

The final night of that trip the students rode a tour bus around the Mall, visiting the illuminated white marble monuments. Their last stop was the Lincoln Memorial, and the Wall.

She climbed the steps of Lincoln's temple, chatting with her best friend. But inside, beneath the statue's grave gaze, reading his words, a solemn mood fell. Afterward, standing beside the reflecting pool, Lily looked across toward the Washington Monument. The gleaming spear floated in the surface of the water. Earlier that day everyone else had ridden the elevator to the top while Lily, afraid of heights, remained below.

Their guide oriented them to the Wall, showed them the registers — thick, chained to podiums: guidebooks to the names of the dead.

What was her father's name? Was he alive or was he inscribed on the dark gleaming surface?

And who was her mother? What was her name? Had he even known? Did anyone know?

Home from the trip, she almost asked about her birth parents. But her imminent graduation from high school and pending departure for college provoked an uneasy season. Soon after she returned from the

Washington field trip, her father moved out — the first of what became a series of trial separations and reconciliations. Asking questions about her origins risked further de-stabilizing things, inflicting more pain on her mother. Protective reticence and silence hardened into habit. She nursed a covert fascination with everything Vietnamese.

Lily met Lam the year she started social work school. The International House on campus advertised a Vietnamese New Year's Party open to all. Dressed in her favorite black silk jacket, wearing her lucky jade earrings, she paused on the threshold of the big lounge — overwhelmed by an incomprehensible cascade of sharp, animated conversation. In a crowd almost exclusively Asian she recognized herself as half-caste imposter. What if someone addressed her in Vietnamese?

At that hesitant moment, Lam appeared and rescued her. Offering a beer, he introduced himself in English — to her grateful relief. A diminutive Vietnamese woman glided up. She wore traditional dress; the slit sides of her long tailored coat revealed a flash of narrow cerise trousers. Lily felt silly, masquerading in Chinatown jacket and jade. The woman stood beside Lam with a proprietary flicker in her eyes. Declining the beer, Lily left the party.

The next day, studying at a long table in the Harper reading room, she felt a tap on her shoulder. She turned and discovered Lam. They walked to the Oriental Institute and spent the afternoon in quiet, empty galleries. Though Lily stared into display cases filled with papyrus scrolls and tomb treasures, she only studied Lam's reflection in the glass: his face was hers — perfected. She wanted him from that moment; claimed him as her birthright.

Over pizza at the Medici he explained the woman at the party was his eldest sister's friend. He'd been dating her on and off, nothing exclusive.

"I'm an only child," Lily said. "I don't share." She meant to sound casual, teasing.

"You won't have to," he said.

He came home with her that night, to her studio apartment carved out of the third floor of a retired professor's house. Her bed stood so close to the elevated rail tracks behind the house it was like making love aboard a train.

What began there led them here, to this night in their shared apartment. She lay in bed and listened to the tap of computer keys from the kitchen. Moving in together in the fall, they had spoken of marriage — but not since. Lily drowsed, imagining a wedding in Rockefeller Chapel, snow falling outside . . . No, not in the chapel . . . A cloud of incense wafts up to the Gothic vault of the Harper reading room as she walks toward him garbed in a bridal scarlet *ao dai*.

Lily awoke to morning shining through the sheet stretched across the window. Parrots squawked outside on the wires. Despite the utility company's efforts to eradicate the messy nests the green birds — descendants of pet store escapees — survived through the cold Chicago winters.

Beside the window, Lam greeted the day, bowing and stretching. Even in too-loose sweats, his slow movements looked elegant. The kettle whistled; he padded barefoot from the room and returned with a mug of green tea. Lily had almost forsworn coffee since living with him.

"Come here," she said, wanting him to return to bed. His reserve always attracted her: making love, breaking through the cool exterior, was like cracking a safe. Lily liked to make him lose control and then lose control herself. She could tell him about the baby — afterward, across the pillow.

"I have to get going." His kissed her, close-mouthed, and stepped away. She jumped up and hit his back. The thud of her fist on his hard shoulder startled them.

"What's that for?" he asked, spinning around.

Her hand burned. She'd never done this before.

"For ignoring me."

"Don't be such a child."

He packed his bag for the library. At the last moment she followed — angry, but reluctant to let him leave without her. They cycled single-file along the Midway past Rockefeller Chapel. Lam liked to climb its tower to the carillon; Lily's vertigo kept her anchored below.

In December they would graduate in the chapel in the small mid-year ceremony.

At the library, Lam locked the bicycles and helmets to a single stanchion. The intimacy of their two machines leaning together reassured her. Claiming their favorite study room, Lam spread his notes across one side of the table. Lily plugged in her laptop; it sang its wake-up song. She shuffled her note cards. The glass library chamber felt pressurized, cut off from the real world outside; her jagged feelings ricocheted off the clear walls.

Lily tossed the cards on the table after a few minutes, like a poker player giving up the game. "I'm going to get my nails done," she said.

"We just got here." Lam radiated disapproval.

"They get busy later."

The nail salon was an extravagance on a student budget, but she was vain about her delicate hands — the one part of her that looked pure Vietnamese. The tiny shop had only two stations and a pedicure chair covered in cracked vinyl. Vietnamese music played on the radio; in the shrine beside the magazine rack a red plastic Buddha presided over offerings of fruit and a stick of incense. The technician wore a jade circle nestled in the hollow of her clavicle.

Lily liked to practice her Vietnamese here, just please and thank you and weather talk. She studied with Rosetta Stone, secretly, on the nights Lam taught. Memory was laid down in language, she had heard at a lecture on international adoption. She wished learning Vietnamese would unlock something forgotten, but thus far it had just proved strange and difficult. After each lesson she rewarded herself with Pepperidge Farm cookies and chocolate milk — alien pleasures in their Vietnamese kitchen but comfort foods of her childhood. For Christmas, she planned to surprise Lam with a conversation. He spoke Vietnamese with his sisters, shutting her out. The sisters disapproved of her; they wanted him to marry their friend, the Vietnamese woman he'd dated before Lily. "Don't take it personally," he said. "It's only cultural. I'm the youngest and they expect to act as my parents, choose my bride.

But I make my own decisions."

His sisters acted as though they were all still squeezed into a small boat together, with Lily an uninvited passenger. The sisters would push her overboard if they could.

The technician squirted lotion on the cuticles and put Lily's hands to soak in the bowl filled with glass pebbles. "You have good week?"

"Yes. You?"

"My baby has first birthday. We have big party. In my country, first birthday very important. We give baby choice — pen, scissor, calculator, chopsticks. He choose what will be."

It required a moment to understand. "When he grows up?"

"He pick pen. Will be good student."

"What do the other things mean?"

"Scissor — barber. Calculator — money, maybe doctor, banker. Chopsticks — good cook."

The manicurist massaged Lily's hands with warm lotion, stretching and pushing the skin as though easing off a glove. This was the best part. A photo of the woman's son was tucked into the Plexiglas frame holding her hygienist's license. He had a pale saucer face beneath a crest of black hair.

"I'm going to have a baby." She said the words for the first time; making the manicurist the first person to know.

The woman looked up. "Congratulations! When?"

"July, I think." Saying the date made it real.

Lily dried her nails, holding them before the fan, inhaling the mingled scent of nail varnish and incense, fighting a ripple of nausea. She imagined Lam — serious, intent — arranging the implements for their baby's birthday fortune-telling. Lily had never known anyone she was related to by blood. Her adoptive parents were big and blond but her baby would look like her, mixed with Lam. She would be able to inventory the baby's features and claim what belonged to her.

Careful not to smudge the fresh varnish, she paid the manicurist. "*Cam o 'n,*" she said, thanking her. "Goodbye. *Chao.*"

Lam did not glance up from his work but wrinkled his nose as though bothered by the smell of nail polish. She poured tea into the thermos cap and tore open a sugar. *Look with favor on a bold beginning,* said the motto on the packet. The tea scalded her throat.

Untimely perhaps, but Lam would not tell her to get rid of it — not after losing his parents, his brother, in the South China Sea.

She typed the website address, furtively as if it was pornography: *AmerVietReunion.net.*

Clicking and scrolling, she selected *FAQ.*

What happens if my father does not want to see or hear from me?

The following day they went to Evanston for dinner with her parents.

Her mother waved from the porch. "There you are! I was starting to worry."

"Perilous, but we managed," said Lam under his breath, unclipping his seat belt.

"Stop," snapped Lily. Lam had picked up her father's sarcastic deprecation of her mother. Awed by the older man's reputation in their shared field, psychology, he admired him — too much. Lily used to tease Lam that he stayed with her to be close to her father.

He used to retort she chose him because she wanted to be Vietnamese.

Dinner was delicious: osso bucco, fennel and orange salad, and pear clafouti for dessert. Sparkling cider instead of wine — her father was on the wagon. Lily operated like a seismograph sensing the shifting plates beneath the surface of her parents' relationship. That evening her father played the genial host, building a fire after dinner. Her mother's face beneath her perennial careful hairstyle, the now graying crown of braids, appeared almost calm. Still, it all seemed provisional. *Contents under pressure.*

"Let's go downstairs. I've set up the projector in the rec room. Thought we'd show Lam some of the old movies," her father said after coffee before the fire.

Downstairs felt cold and clammy, with the damp plaster smell she remembered from when the basement room had been her high-school hangout. Her mother plugged in the space heater. Lily curled up next to Lam under the afghan, on the old convertible couch — the couch where she lost her virginity. She rubbed her hand along the Naugahyde cushion, remembering the sting of the plastic surface against her bare, sun-burnt back, her boyfriend's skin tasting of sweat and suntan cream and chlorine.

"Lights, Lam," said her father. The projector whirred.

Her father appeared on the screen — young, crew-cut, gazing square into the camera through heavy black-framed glasses.

"Me, as a post-doc," he said. "Ready to unlock the mysteries of the universe."

The camera panned to what resembled a large checkered ping pong table with a board lying flat across the surface instead of a net.

"Okay, here you have it! Dress rehearsal time," Lily's father said. "That's the proto-type set up, the very first simulated drop-off."

"The false precipice," said Lam reverently. "So simple. Brilliant."

"Well, I don't know about brilliant, but I'll grant you the simple. Just a sheet of heavy glass three feet off the ground with a board down the middle and high-contrast cloth underneath."

"I found the checked fabric," said her mother. "On sale."

Lily did not recall hearing that detail before though she had seen this film a million times. Like any student in Psych 101, she knew the checked cloth glued flush to the underside of the glass on one side of the board-divider created the illusion of solidity. On the other side, the same fabric was stretched out on the ground beneath the table, to deceive. A baby looking down through the clear glass perceived a sheer drop. A precipice.

Back on screen, her young father positioned a squirming black-haired baby on the bridge-board.

"There's Lily, seven months old. Just starting to crawl when we got her. Perfect timing."

The baby rocked on hands and knees, in crawl position. The camera panned across the glass expanse to her slender mother, face tense beneath signature crown of braids, lips moving. Even without a sound-track, across the years, Lily heard her mother call her to cross over.

The camera switched back to Lily. The baby gingerly reached out a dimpled hand and patted the glass. She gazed toward her mother but didn't venture off the board.

"See, soon as they begin to crawl, they're developing depth perception. Risk avoidance. Doesn't look safe. She's not going to chance it."

The baby's round face crumpled, crying.

Watching herself on screen Lily felt a catch in her chest like incipient panic.

Her mother re-appeared, picking up the baby, cradling her.

"I don't know who was more upset, me or Lily," her mother said as the film flickered and ended.

"So why'd you let him use me?" Lily was enraged. It had never hit her like this before.

Her father chuckled as though she joked. "Whole set-up was safe, but you're right. Today we'd have to jump through hoops with the human subjects review board. I should probably add a disclaimer to this movie — no babies were harmed, etcetera, etcetera."

Lam laughed also, too hard, like someone making up to the boss. "Now I know why Lily's scared of heights."

"Did it make a difference, that I was adopted? Maybe I didn't know who Mom was yet. Maybe I would have risked it, if I did," Lily said.

"That's Lam's department. Attachment."

"Interesting question," said Lam. "Did anyone ever run any comparison studies — with adoptive and biological babies and mothers?"

"Nope. All yours, if you dare brave the ethics committee."

"No way, sir. They'd be all over the classic attachment experiments now. Bowlby wouldn't have a chance."

"Or Ainsworth. Mother leaves the baby in the playroom and a stranger comes in?"

"Phenomenal work. I've seen the footage. Definitely reminds

me of the way the baby in your experiment reacted to the cues to danger, separation from the attachment object."

Lily interrupted. "It's me you're talking about."

"More coffee anyone?" asked her mother, fluttering up from the chair, turning on the lights.

Upstairs, the fire had burnt out. Lam's cell phone rang. He glanced at the display and then across the room to Lily. "My sister," he said and let it go to voice mail. Lily felt something like victory. Perhaps he was beginning to understand what she meant about setting limits with his sisters.

Lam's phone rang again. His jaw tightened.

"Someone really wants you," said her father.

"Excuse me," Lam said and stepped out of the room, opening his phone.

Lily followed him into the hallway, disappointed he'd weakened, given in again. This was her night, their night with her family.

"Tell her you'll call later," she hissed.

He waved her away.

Dismissed, she went into the kitchen. Her mother stood at the sink, filling the coffeepot with water.

Angry at Lam, her father, she burst out. "I need to know who my birth parents are — were. It matters to Lam, his sisters have been asking." A lie — no possible pedigree could win his family's approval.

Her mother flinched; her hand shook. Water splashed.

"The Sisters at the orphanage didn't know who left you."

It should have come as no surprise, but she felt betrayed — like waking up that time on the train from Paris to Milan robbed of wallet and passport.

"So how did you know how old I was?" Lily heard her voice — petulant, accusing.

The espresso pot spit and sputtered; her mother adjusted the flame.

"The Sisters estimated. Your pediatrician thought it was close enough."

"Any hope of coffee?" asked her father from the doorway.

Glaring at him, Lily pushed past. In the hall, Lam murmured into the phone, hand cupped over his mouth, oblivious.

Lily cleared her throat.

Startled, he glanced up; his expression guarded. Guilty.

And for the second time in moments she felt robbed, betrayed. He was speaking to a girlfriend, not his sister.

Grabbing the phone away, Lily shouted into it. *"Chao-chi! Chao-chi!"*

She surprised him; she surprised herself with her mastery.

"What's going on out here?" Her father held the coffee tray; her mother peered around his bulk.

"We have to leave," said Lily.

"Thank you for dinner," said Lam to her mother, formal and correct. "And for showing me the film, sir. An honor to know you." Staking a claim on her father, no matter what.

Lam drives too fast.

Lily leans her head against the car window. When she was little, she had an imaginary friend. But the baby is real: her secret creation, her only blood kin.

The wipers erase the snow from the windshield. The window becomes a black mirror, swallowing her reflection. Lily sees her baby on the other side of the glass, crawling across the windshield precipice, looking in. Looking for her.

Lily closes her eyes. She stands in her father's lab, at the edge of the false cliff, holding the baby. And the baby holds her; they protect each other.

The wipers hiss and sigh, like breathing.

Sea Change

Adrienne swam before she walked, snorkeled at six.

"What do you want to be when you grow up?" the grown-ups asked.

"A deep sea diver."

In high school her family called her an amphibious creature crossed with a book worm, more interested in fish and reading than in boys. Not altogether true — she dated the captain of the high school swim team (skinny, hairless tadpole, all shoulders and legs) until out-swimming and humiliating him. She discovered you can't cry underwater, swam solitary healing laps, and lay in the sun, reading Jacques Cousteau and Jules Verne.

At New College, Adrienne spent more time in Sarasota Bay than in class. Researching her senior honors thesis — echolocation in dolphins — she met a schooner bum and after graduation sailed the Caribbean with him. In Surinam, returning with groceries from the market, she found him in their bunk with a woman from a cruise ship. Adrienne flew back to the States and graduate school at Berkeley where, in the Department's submersible vessel, she studied clouds of fluffy green phytodetritus, finding even the waste from phytoplankton beautiful. She wrote her dissertation on the *Yolidia* clam's use of a small, mysterious appendage to detect the chemical state of its environment.

Friends married — on beaches and ship decks, in vineyards and redwood circles. She felt wistful but despite a few brief affairs, nothing stuck; she found no one as seductive as the secret world beneath the surface of the water, no late-night assignation satisfying as the midnight lab illuminated by the iridescent green of her aquariums. By the time she received her hood and doctorate, some friends (already on a second child or second marriage) had dropped out of the game to teach high school science, work for pharmaceuticals. Adrienne's clams, plankton, and algae required her full complement of nurture. "My significant other is named *Yolidia*," she said, refusing fix-up dates and introductions.

She turned down a tenure track professorship at San Diego State for the Oceanographic Institute at Woods Hole. The position offered field work on mollusks *in situ*, and housing on the beach. Adrienne bought a sailboat and practically lived in her wetsuit, swimming even in rough winter surf.

The marine snail *Aplysia* captured her attention. Its response to threat — increased heart rate and jets of ink — convinced Adrienne that the primitive mollusk experienced something like fear. The lab chief, Polly, encouraged her to write up the findings and submit a paper for publication.

Shop talk in the lab and the canteen sufficed for company. She skipped lab parties, avoided informal potlucks and the occasional communal "culture runs" to Boston. Evenings, after checking the temperature of her tanks, she wandered through the public display rooms overrun with tourist families and field-tripping children by day. Alone in the aqueous light, she peered in at ancient lobsters and horseshoe crabs, pitying them, living out their days there instead of on the ocean floor. She felt kin to the captive specimens; even working and living so close to the water, she yearned. Adrienne envied astronauts' lengthy sojourns on space stations in the heavens.

On winter Sundays she made pots of soup big and deep enough to last the week, and read Thoreau's journal of his visit to the Cape in 1857 and Henry Beston's *Outermost House*. Beston understood: "The world today is sick to its thin blood for lack of elemental things."

One snowy January evening, snug before the fire, catching up on professional journals, a classified ad in *The Review of Experimental Biology* caught her eye. "Seeking adventurous scientist for underwater exploration. Willingness to relocate a prerequisite."

Awakening in the middle of the night, she called the number. "You have reached Dr. Jonah Larsen at Massachusetts General Hospital," said the tape. Jonah Larsen, a familiar name, one of the pioneers in work with hormones and sex change surgery. What was he up to now?

The next morning she reached his secretary.

"Would you like a Prospective Subjects Questionnaire?"

"I'd like to know about the project first."

"Due to the highly sensitive nature of the research, Dr. Larsen will only be able to provide a study description to accepted applicants."

"Well, I'm certainly not applying if I don't know what I'm applying for," Adrienne said, crumpling the ad and tossing it in the wastebasket.

But she retrieved the scrap of paper before leaving for work, and tucked it inside the leather cover of her day planner. On her coffee break, she stepped outside. Shivering in the damp cold air, watching a ferry plough through the white caps toward Martha's Vineyard, she flipped open her phone.

The Prospective Subjects Questionnaire arrived; the cover letter confirmed a study description would be provided "only to those applicants selected for in person interviews." The mystery exerted an irresistible lure. No harm in completing the paperwork, if only to discover what the hush-hush protected.

Documenting her professional background required more space than entering the personal data. Non-smoking, no medications, no chronic health conditions. Single. No children. Pregnant? Prior pregnancies? No. None.

References? The bold print promised no one would be contacted at this preliminary stage but she couldn't risk Polly. Her dissertation advisor would do, warned and prepped beforehand. Probably nothing would come of it anyway. She sealed the envelope and posted it — excited, as though tossing a message in a bottle out to sea.

"I am pleased to invite you for an intake interview. Call to schedule at your earliest convenience." An indecipherable signature scrawled across the heavy cream page. No study prospectus; Larsen still withheld the bait.

"I have to go into Boston," she told Polly, not volunteering any explanation. "Sorry it's such short notice — only for the day."

"Everything OK?"

"Just a personal matter."

Her boss worked long hours across the hall. Like children engaged in parallel play, they shared an unspoken intimacy and protected each other's privacy.

"Leave me instructions by your tanks, for feeding and temperature checks."

Jonah Larsen had likely been handsome once, and still looked distinguished with his patrician bald brow, nose strong and beaked as a Medici's. He interrogated her for over two hours, reviewing her pedigree in marine biology, but spending more time on the personal history. Her open water swimming seemed to impress him more than her research.

He stared at her with pale blue eyes — the color of water in the rocky tide pools of the beaches of the Pacific Northwest. Did she have a boyfriend? Any intention of having children? Illegal questions, if she'd been a job applicant. No and no, she answered, swallowing fury at his trespass.

The fat envelope arrived on Valentine's Day.

"We are pleased to inform you of your selection from a highly competitive pool of applicants. Please read the enclosed protocol. Should you for any reason choose to decline this invitation, you remain bound by the statement of confidentiality executed at your interview. Call to schedule your intake appointment at your earliest convenience."

Adrienne opened the booklet (*Distribution and duplication prohibited*) and began to read.

As is often the case in science, a seeming coincidence led to the present inquiry. The serendipity in this instance is my work as an endocrinological consultant at Massachusetts General Hospital, one of the few institutions in the world performing separation surgeries on individuals with the rare congenital condition Sirenomelia, or "Mermaid's Syndrome".

Sirens, Larsen explained, have fused legs. In most, blood vessels cross from side to side of the circulatory system, precluding separation surgery. Even after successful leg separation, former sirens require extensive hormone therapy in addition to physical therapy to develop the capacity to ambulate more or less normally.

In addition to serving as consultant to separation surgeons, I have participated in the General's longitudinal follow-up studies of former sirens. A striking, unexpected, and most intriguing qualitative finding is that even years after successful surgery, some former sirens report persistent sensory confusion: a tactile hallucination, a feeling they **still have a tail** *— rather like the well-known "phantom limb" syndrome in amputees. These individuals further describe feeling uncomfortable in their bipedal bodies, and many say they feel like "fish out of water." This phenomenon, reminiscent of the dilemma of transgendered patients, inspires my present research interest in the novel, highly experimental field of Trans-species Reassignment Therapy. Subjects in the proposed experimental study will receive hormone therapy directed to the goal of affecting a complete reverse metamorphosis. The successful study subject may expect to become fully aquatic, capable of living underwater: to* **devolve** *from mammal to amphibian and finally, become an Aquanaut.*

The intake appointment required an in-patient stay.

"I need a few days off, just till Wednesday," she told Polly. Adrienne's bi-weekly pay stub showed an astronomical balance of accrued annual and sick days.

"You'll arrange for someone to do the feeding, take the samples for you?" asked Polly. (Not offering, Adrienne noticed, to do it herself.) The world-renowned oceanographer had always treated Adrienne more as peer than subordinate. But now the reed-thin, grey-haired woman pressed her lips together and turned away.

It's science. Nothing frivolous, Adrienne wanted to protest.

Trapped in the stale air of the waiting room, listening to muzak, Adrienne watched goldfish circle a bowl on the reception desk. Her palms sweated, her heart pounded. Just nerves, she told herself. Calm down. Finally, a nurse holding a clipboard appeared.

"Leave your clothes and purse in the locker. Tie the gown so it opens in the front."

She waited another long interval in an examining room, shivering in the flimsy paper robe. "He's hazing me," she thought. But when the room went dark, she panicked and jumped from the table.

The light flicked on. Adrienne caught her breath, embarrassed. Of course, energy efficient lights on a timer, extinguished by stillness, activated by movement.

"Ready?" asked the nurse, opening the door.

Mammogram, EKG, blood work, urinalysis, vitals, reflexes, PET scan, CT scan, MRIs: a thorough going-over. During the pelvic exam's routine humiliation (feet spread in useless stirrups, Larsen's gloved hand probing) she imagined fused legs, a neutered state, and flinched. She stared into the fluorescent ceiling tiles and chanted silently *the successful study subject may expect to become fully aquatic, capable of living under water.*

"You may get dressed now," said the nurse.

A battery of psychological tests followed, administered by a young woman with protuberant eyes like a *Pricanthus arenatus* (but excellent legs, very excellent bipedal appendages, in fishnet stockings beneath her short white coat). Adrienne looked down at her own legs — strong and long. Necessary sacrifice, but she'd miss them.

Finally, a five page consent form detailed risks and benefits, possible side effects, probable irreversible change, certain deformity, a chance of death, the possibility of being assigned to the control group on placebo. "The successful study subject may expect to become fully aquatic, capable of living under water," she reminded herself, signing on the dotted line.

Dr. Larsen's severe nurse instructed her in the medication regime and warned against shaving her legs (due to the risk of nicking the anticipated subcutaneous layer of scales).

Adrienne tapped on the fishbowl on the reception counter as the gum-chewing secretary scheduled her follow up appointments. She filled her prescriptions at the hospital's basement pharmacy and drove home on automatic pilot, her copy of the waiver locked in the glove compartment, pills rattling in her handbag. That evening, the last long night of the short month of February, she swallowed her first dose.

By St. Patrick's Day the pussy willows in the sheltered corner by the garage were beginning to swell and fuzz. Like a pre-pubescent girl longing for breasts, Adrienne studied herself daily in the mirror after bathing, looking for changes, for some sign of the hoped for metamorphosis. Nothing. She grew impatient with everyone, everything — the lab, Woods Hole, the scientists and fishermen, the insular community felt stifling. Even her clams and snails ceased to delight her. Every night she walked along the beach and gazed into the dark water.

She requested sick leave for the first monthly follow-up. Polly quivered with curiosity — like an anemone waving suspicious tentacles.

Larsen pinned her X-rays, her scans, to the light board in the examining room: nothing.

She pressed him. When might she expect evidence of the change? What would the first indicator be? Due to the experimental nature of the procedure, he couldn't say, but the first sign might be webbing, between the toes and fingers. Not long after that, visible scales should appear, her legs fuse, and the gills develop.

"Any dreams?" asked the psychologist in the required counseling session.

"No," lied Adrienne.

"None?" insisted the woman, bulging eyes studying her as though reading her mind like a slide in a microscope.

Adrienne confessed the recent nightmare — a flashback to almost drowning once, back in Sarasota. She'd been training for free immersion deep diving, eager to attempt what divers call the most dangerous event in the world, to descend hundreds of feet on one breath. But on her first dive, she blacked out. Afraid to try again, she sold the expensive mono-fin. Now the aborted exploit felt like an omen.

Anticipatory anxiety, the therapist suggested (dismissive, condescending). Quite a common phenomenon. But if she'd changed her mind, wanted to see if there was any chance of turning back, she must talk to Larsen immediately.

Certainly not, said Adrienne.

She missed a deadline for a grant; couldn't finish the abstract on her findings regarding *Aplysia* and evoked emotion. The heater in one of her tanks failed and plankton floated to the surface, limp and brown. Adrienne filed the required incident report.

Polly summoned her. "NOAA's coming for the accreditation site visit this fall. Your grant is up for renewal. We can't afford sloppy work, any careless mistakes. You know how tight money is under this administration. I'm not formally putting you on probation, but I need two hundred percent from everyone."

"I'm sorry."

"And I want you to join the lab team for the Coney Island Parade this year. We're going as the Global Warming Mermaids."

"I need to stay here, focus on my work."

"You *need* to fully participate in the life of the lab, Adrienne. We *need* esprit de corps to get through accreditation."

Adrienne, ashamed as though she'd been called to the principal's office, retreated to her lab. The neat columns of data in her log book shimmered through a scrim of angry tears. She needed the escape of metamorphosis. Soon.

Spring advanced: dune grass furred the sand with a haze of olive. Clamorous, northward bound geese filled the sky. Locals stroked fresh paint on shutters, preparing for summer tenants. Adrienne swam morning and night; going in without her wet suit, hoping to discover she'd grown able to tolerate the cold, searching for a sign. Shivering, skin mottled and blue, she crawled out on the beach. *Accept it. You're just a control.*

Parade day, arms linked, Adrienne and the Global Warming Mermaids minced along in tight spandex tails, a chorus line of amphibious Rockettes accompanied by a brass band of pirates blasting *Yellow*

Submarine. The sun set and beyond the boardwalk fireworks exploded into dusk. King Neptune, a massive wrestler slathered in silver body paint and festooned with garlands of seaweed, waved from his throne beneath the Ferris wheel. Adrienne broke free, cursing as she tripped over her tail, struggling through a school of little girl jelly fish in gauzy capes and stumbling down the stairs to the beach.

The detritus of the revelers lay scattered on the sand: Mardi Gras beads, plastic tridents, cloth leis. Adrienne unzipped her tail, peeled it off, stashed it under the steps and strode toward the water in her bikini, enjoying the damp sea-spray on her bare legs, celebrating release from the silly costume. An inviting path of moonlight stretched from the shore. She plunged in.

A seal surfaced. No, a man's sleek head, powerful shoulders.

"Hey," he called. "For a moment I thought you were a mermaid."

They swam together, along the shoreline, then waded in and walked back toward the lights. She admired his muscular legs.

"So you are a mermaid," he laughed when Adrienne retrieved her tail from beneath the boardwalk. "What about some dinner?"

"I'm cold, I have to find my friends, get the car keys for my clothes."

"I have sweats and a towel under the next set of stairs. Borrow my stuff. I'll go for carry-out. Sushi OK?"

They took turns with the flimsy chopsticks — he'd only brought back one set. The wasabi stung her nose and she coughed just as he kissed her the first time.

After eating, sitting on his damp towel on sand radiating cold, they kissed again until she pulled away — unsettled by the sensation between her legs. Just attraction or, finally, metamorphosis beginning? Adrienne tried not to think, tried just to want him. Once, she might have. Her teenage self might have crawled under the boardwalk and just done it, ignoring the grit of the sand, a little turned on by the noise of the crowd above.

"Ever notice how you see the moon in the water first, before the sky?" she asked, apologetic, embarrassed.

"Sure, physics, and Buddhism," he said. Tarn knew about both, he explained, as a physicist and practicing Buddhist, doing a post-doc at MIT.

Timing is everything, she reflected ruefully. He might have been interesting to get to know, if they'd met before.

Curled up in the lab van on the long drive north back to Cape Cod, Adrienne dreamed — not of Tarn, but of diving, alone, effortless and deep. At the bottom, on a shadowed ocean floor, she swam swishing her tail and fins. Waking in the bleached artificial light of a turnpike rest stop, she wondered: if she were a fish, would she dream of land? Always what she couldn't have?

Tarn e-mailed, inviting himself for a visit. Adrienne composed a response, claiming a pressing grant deadline, deferring a visit into some unspecified future moment. Her finger hovered over the "Send" command. Perhaps she should try it, one more time. One last time? Perhaps he was her consolation prize, for being trapped in this body, marooned in the terrestrial world.

Deleting her careful message she wrote: *How about the weekend of the Fourth? There'll be fireworks.* She clicked "send" and regretted it immediately.

He arrived on the bus from Boston. She'd never seen him by daylight, dry, and fully clothed. He looked shorter, barrel-chested, disproportionate. Hair curled over his collar.

At the fish market, he selected lobster bodies and offered to make bisque. Adrienne didn't confess she'd lost her appetite for rich chowders; she craved miso broth and kelp salad, periwinkles on the side. She bicycled to the farm stand for corn and came back to her own kitchen polluted by clouds of milky, salty steam.

But after dinner, they swam by starlight, fingers trailing reflected phosphorescent constellations, treading water, watching the blinking of the buoys, the purposeful lights of the Vineyard ferry. His curls looked sleek as fur in the water and she could once again imagine him a seal, an otter. They showered together under the rough spray of the outdoor shower and made love in her loft bedroom. The beacon of the lighthouse shone in her window, washing over the bed like water. He fell asleep, anchoring her under a heavy arm. She rolled away and crept out alone to wade on the beach.

The next day after dispatching him on the Peter Pan bus, Adrienne ran a deep bubble bath and soaked until the water cooled — but her skin did not pucker. Drying off, she discovered a tiny flap of webbing between her toes. Her heart somersaulted. Dialing Larsen's hotline, she quivered with excitement and terror. This must be what her friends described, when a pregnancy test read positive.

Ordered to Boston immediately, Adrienne left her resignation letter on the soapstone lab bench. She stared into her tanks and tapped a Morse code goodbye on the glass. Halfway down the hall, she turned back, scooped her clams and snails into a bucket, carried them out to the Institute dock, and released the *Yolidia* and *Aplysia* to the sea.

Larsen examined her, his eyes sparkling. On the illuminated x-rays Adrienne saw a ghostly layer of scales beneath her skin.

"Excellent," Larsen said, as she trembled in the paper gown in the air-conditioned cell of the examining room. He froze her with his pale blue gaze — the flat, emotionless glance of the great white shark she'd encountered once, diving off Baja. "You'll be admitted as an inpatient, for the duration."

Adrienne walked along Charles Street, staring in the dusty windows of the antique shops at relics of earthly domestic life — sherry glasses, porcelain ginger jars. She drank a brandy at the Ritz before calling Tarn.

"I'm in town," she said.

"Great! Come out for dinner. Spend the night."

"No," she said. "I can't stay. Come in. Meet me at the swan boats."

Almost dinner time, the tourists and children and mothers

33

dispersed. One solitary swan boat toiled around the pond. Tarn and Adrienne rode alone on the front bench.

She explained, speaking softly, though the bored young man piloting their swan wore earphones.

Tarn snorted in disbelief. "If you don't want to see me, just say so. Spare me the tall tales."

"No," she said. "It's true." And extended her hand and spread her fingers, revealing the webbing, new since morning, which already reached almost to her first knuckle.

He stared. "There's got to be an antidote."

"It's what I wanted," she said.

"Before," he said, earnest and serious, brown eyes deep and soft as a seal's. "Do you want it still?" He touched her cheek with a hot, dry hand.

She hesitated. Did she want it still? She almost could imagine a future with him, working in a little college along the coast of Maine, teaching their own school of tan, brown-haired water babies to swim (in tiny wetsuits buoyed by fluorescent orange water wings).

Adrienne looked into the shallow murk lapping past the awkward boat. A hopeful duck paddled and quacked in the wake; a crumpled soda cup floated by.

"I'm sorry," she said. "It's too late."

Larsen prescribed bed rest at Mass General. By week's end, a thin layer of glittering green scales girdled her hips and belly. She broke the rules, tried to get up to go to the bathroom alone, and fell. Her legs had fused. A nurse came running, and called Dr. Larsen.

"Wonderful," he said, rubbing his pale hands together — the fingers long as the stinging tentacles of a jelly fish. He palpated her throat with his chilly fingers, as though checking for swollen glands. "Good, good — that's likely a bit sensitive, isn't it? Your gill ventricles are opening, my dear. Now, I'm putting a tag with a tracking chip in it on your ear."

"A tracking chip?" She didn't recall that, from the consent forms.

"To keep tabs on you. Just a little pinch — there. We'll move you to the Aquarium on the harbor tonight."

"The Aquarium?"

"We're using one of their boats, with a holding tank. If you do O.K., submerged overnight, we'll take you to the Cape and release you tomorrow."

Lying in bed, impatient as a kidnap victim in her strange hybrid body, Adrienne imagined the sea. She yearned for freedom, to swim away. *Is this like dying? Everything left behind, burnt away by readiness?*

That evening, an orderly lifted her from bed to gurney. They rode a freight elevator down and rolled through labyrinthine miles of underground corridors, finally surfacing in a parking garage. The orderly loaded the gurney inside the waiting ambulance.

"Let's go," Dr. Larsen shouted from the driver's seat.

Adrienne gasped; the caustic air seared through her gills.

A cargo net dropped Adrienne into the ship's tank. Water flowed over her gills like cool spring air. Beyond the glass wall, she could see the gleam of Dr. Larsen's white coat. She closed her eyes and sank to the bottom and slept.

In the morning, the boat's engine groaned to life; water in the tank sloshed, rocking Adrienne back and forth. The ship churned out into the harbor, then beyond, into open sea.

Netted, hoisted up out of the tank, she swung out over the edge of the boat in a wild hammock ride. And then, released, she plummeted into the ocean. Down, down, down on a single breath. Free immersion diving at last. She drifted through a forest of seaweed without effort, without fear. Stretching, wriggling what had been her toes, fluttering her tail, she floated to the surface.

Sunbeams refracted by the water above dazzled her with shards of rainbows like a celestial chandelier. She vaulted out of the water and splashed down, exhilarated. A seal surfaced beside her; its smooth, dark head, liquid brown eyes reminded her of something. The faint, indistinct memory slipped away as a school of dolphins nuzzled her, chortling, winking. The mermaid flipped her powerful tail and joined the frolic, leaping up, splashing down into the bottle green sea.

Peripheral Vision

Halloween falls the weekend before Election Day. "Come as a political character!" the invitation says.

"Who shall we be?" asks Walker. Meg's husband assumes they're going, and going as a couple. She's teetered on the cusp of leaving him all fall. He seems oblivious, surely grounds enough for leaving.

At night in bed, stiff as a carved stone figure on a sarcophagus, he sleeps while resentment rises and hangs above her, like steam off a compost pile on a winter morning. Younger, angry with him, she could drop through the escape hatch of sleep into dreams of sex with her old boyfriend. Now, she doesn't sleep so easily, and doesn't feel sexy even in dreams. Wakeful, tense, she walks through their house in her imagination and inventories the contents of each room, labeling the furniture and artifacts of their marriage for some apocalyptic yard sale. Carving up their shared lives would be delicate as separating Siamese twins joined at the heart.

Like the Count of Monte Cristo, like an inmate on death row, she surreptitiously digs and chips her way out of the house, the life — starting with her closet, filling bags with clothes she's too old or heavy or sad to ever wear again. How subjective the line is, between trash and treasure, Meg thinks, stuffing a beaded black dress into a bulging grocery bag for the thrift shop.

Christ Episcopal Church runs the Bargain Box; its proceeds support the homeless shelter. The shop is really like a box — stuffed with the detritus of an affluent congregation in the throes of an epidemic of house cleaning, or divorce. After turning in her cast-offs and receiving the tax receipt, Meg trolls the aisles.

On a folding table littered with china and candy dishes and chipped figurines, she finds them: the Kennedys, Jack and Jackie. The celluloid masks are vintage souvenirs; the original price tags still stuck inside: 39 cents.

Holding the brittle masks gingerly, she scans the racks for a simple sheath: brocade, or silk. She'll wear her mother's white gloves and pearls.

It almost jumps off the hanger — not a sheath but a suit. Pale pink wool, pencil skirt, and brief boxy jacket with a deep, round collar. Pure sixties, the label reads Peck & Peck. She remembers their elegant black and white ads in *The New Yorker*, when she was a teenager wearing go-go boots and minis. Size eight. It should fit.

"Could you hold these masks for me? I want to try this on," she says to the plump volunteer at the cash register.

"Oh, my goodness," says the woman. "Jack and Jackie."

The skirt's waist is snug, but she can leave the button at the placket undone. The jacket is perfect. Meg preens a moment, admiring how the scoop neck frames her collar bones. Once, long ago, Walker kissed his way along her clavicle. When she was younger, people said she looked like Jackie, or Audrey Hepburn. Maybe it was the long legs, wide eyes, high cheekbones, and her ballet school posture. She'd laughed it off, but been secretly flattered. No one's noticed a resemblance for years, even before both Jackie and Audrey died.

She fastens the buttons — like little blackberries, glistening, glittering against the pale blush wool. Meg can't resist showing off and steps into the shop.

The cashier nods approval. "Fits like it was made for you. And look what I've found!" She holds up a black pill box hat, with a ruffle of veil.

Meg slips the mask on and steps to the mirror, holding the hat.

Her reflection startles her: the stiff celluloid face above the pink suit has come alive. Jackie looks back at her.

"Eerie," the woman says.

Meg smiles, and then remembers her face, her own face, is hidden. "Thanks for finding the hat."

"What did you say?"

The mask distorts her voice; she'll have to speak louder, pitch her words higher. "I'll wear the suit home. Give my husband a surprise."

Meg drives in her sneakers and the pink suit, Jack and Jackie lying on the seat beside her, staring at the ceiling of the car. In the driveway she puts on her mask then rings the doorbell.

"Trick or treat!" she says. "Here's Jack, for you."

It surprises her, how thoroughly he gets into it. Kennedy's nasal voice echoes from the study; she finds her masked husband in front of the computer.

"Listen to this," he says. "It's his inauguration speech, on YouTube. What if I memorize a couple of lines, for the party?"

When did she last see him this light-hearted?

Another scene flickers on the computer screen: footage from Dallas, just before the assassination. Even decades later, it's mesmerizing. Watch out, she wants to shout to the handsome gallant. Duck! Stop waving!

Her earliest political memory is of JFK at a campaign rally. She remembers the excited crowd in the grocery store parking lot on a bitter cold day; she remembers the hot bubble bath afterward.

Now she watches the doomed parade over Walker's shoulder. She made a scrap book of the Kennedy family after the assassination, pasting in pictures from newspapers and magazines. Ten years old, she'd grieved as though it were her own father who'd been killed.

"Turn that off," she says. Their masquerade feels disrespectful. "Maybe it's not such a good idea." Jackie wore a pink suit, too. It ended up blood-stained.

"Lighten up for once. It's only a party."

The chink in the wall closes. It's easier, habit, to be irritated.

Meg searches for the gloves; she can almost feel the raised seam ridges down each finger, the round mother of pearl button at the wrist. Where are they? Not resting in the back of her lingerie drawer, rolled into a neat, quiet ball as she'd expected. Finally she discovers them in the wicker hamper of dress-ups — beneath crumpled tulle skirts, a frizzy clown wig, her discarded slips (Cinderella gowns when sashed with Walker's ties). Both daughters are out of college now, wearing real clothes in real life; she's the one playing dress-up. Isn't that what the magazines prescribe, to reinvigorate the marriage bed?

Meg uses the girls' room as dressing room and walk-in closet. She claimed it when they left, hungry for space and privacy after years of staging her schedule so as not to interfere with Walker's fastidious preparation for work. She completes the transformation into Jackie: blows her hair with gel into a thick bouffant, shortens the pearl strand to choker length (skipping earrings, the mask would hide them). Her black patent pumps are too square heeled for the sixties, but will do.

Maybe the magazines are right. Not that it's sexy she feels, but at least distracted from the tedious grip of resentment. She'd pitied people like the Clintons, Diana and Charles, enduring private problems in the glare of public attention. The Kennedys, too, with Jack and Marilyn. But perhaps state occasions, pretending for an audience, help.

"How do I look?" asks Walker.

He's wearing the gray pin-striped Brooks Brothers suit purchased for their wedding thirty years ago: lapels cut for Reagan not Kennedy, but retro enough.

"It still fits."

"I haven't gained weight, or not that much," he says, huffy.

Friends at reunions exclaim the couple looks the same. The changes are subtle, a spiritual hardening of the arteries.

"Put on your mask," she says, suddenly remembering a rare sex dream she did have, not that long ago. A bondage dream.

He slips it on. "Ask not what your country can do for you — ask what you can do for your country." The muffled imitation isn't good but the woman in the Bargain Box was right: it's eerie.

She puts her mask on and looks in the mirror over the sideboard to fix the hat. Jackie's face leers back at her.

JFK looms over her shoulder. "Let's take a picture," he says. "I'll put the camera on tripod."

As the timer counts down, she starts to smile, then relaxes. It's a relief to let the mask do the work: she's not photogenic, famous for shutting her eyes at the crucial moment, which irritates Walker — as though she's stayed up late, planning how to spoil the picture.

They leave the porch light on and a bowl of Kit Kats and Reese's Cups for trick-or-treaters, though few will come. The neighborhood has grown old.

It's a twenty minute drive to the party, across town on Capitol Hill. Once on the Hill, they encounter barricades and one-way streets: the intentional obstacle course erected since 9/11. Walker fumes. "You couldn't pay me to live at ground zero."

How much would a studio apartment in the attic of one of these townhouses run? It's a transitional neighborhood, but moving in the right direction. She could bike to the Smithsonian.

Finding the curb in front of the party house parked solid, Walker drives two blocks farther before locating a spot in front of a liquor store armored with a metal grill. They walk back quickly, spooked by the deserted street, relieved to reach their hosts' block, tended and prosperous. A jack o' lantern glows on the steps; a plastic skeleton hangs from the potted tree in the courtyard. This couple likes to live large, throwing big parties with lots to drink, sometimes live music. Walker slips on the mask; his narrow face disappears behind florid plastic jowls topped by Jack's pompadour.

Their host opens the door, wearing a plaid shirt, cowboy boots and hat. Is he Reagan or Bush in brush-clearing garb?

"Ask not what your country can do for you, but what you can do for your country," says Walker.

"Wow — Mr. President, Jackie, what an honor. Who's in there?"

He's too drunk to recognize Walker's blurred voice. They're incognito.

The small, high-ceilinged rooms are hot and crowded with milling, mingling guests. Two Sarah Palins face off over a tray of hors d'oeuvres. The Pope sits in a corner, chatting with a giant brown cardboard box labeled "Economic Stimulus Package." A tall androgynous woman in tail coat and top hat scoops up crab dip: Abe Lincoln.

Walker pushes his mask up over his forehead. Meg's face grows moist and sweaty but she keeps the mask on, enjoying invisibility.

"There's a fortune teller in the sunroom upstairs, Jackie," says their hostess, yet another Sarah Palin: the best of the bunch, winking behind her glasses, nailing the naughty librarian look.

"Thanks, Governor," Meg says, trying to sound lock-jawed, finishing school upper-crusty.

There's a line up the stairs for the fortune teller. Meg leans against the balustrade. Below in the foyer, her husband, holding a plate of scallops wrapped in bacon, chats with Queen Elizabeth I. The statuesque redhead was the drama teacher at the girls' school. On the step above her, a man in a hospital Johnny carries an I.V. bag. "The sick economy on life support," he explains. One step down, Monica Lewinsky in a blue dress with a conspicuous stain, talks about her landscape architecture practice to a young man with a noose around his neck and a nametag: "Chad."

The fortune teller spends a long time with each person. Walker pushes up the stairs, jumping the line. "I'm with Jackie," he says to Monica Lewinsky.

"I'm first," Meg says when it's her turn, stepping into the sunroom and closing the door in JFK's face.

The room's a deep alcove in a bay window. She imagines mornings here, alone with a second cup of coffee, the expensive cloth blinds like candled eggshell as light streams in.

"Sit down." The fortune teller's frizzy gray hair escapes from a turban, but even in costume-shop gypsy apparel — gauzy skirt, Mardi Gras beads — she's intimidating. Meg perches on the ottoman opposite the woman's wing chair, conscious of being lower: a supplicant, at a disadvantage.

"Take off your mask," the gypsy orders. The woman makes no other comment on Meg's costume. It's like being in a doctor's examining room: clothes, identity and status rendered irrelevant. "Do you want me to do the cards or read your palm?"

"My palm, please."

"Take off the gloves."

Meg's nervous as she struggles off the gloves. It feels like stripping. She's never had her palm read.

"Which hand do you write with?"

"My right."

The woman holds her hand palm up, studying intently. Meg feels a flicker of fear — like the moment each year just before the mammographer squeezes her breast flat between the plates of glass. She almost pulls away, almost says she's changed her mind.

"So," the gypsy says. "A fire hand."

"Is that good?" asks Meg, glad of the closed door, the confessional privacy.

"You're energetic. Creative. You have a short fuse."

There's only a limited menu of character traits; the accuracy may be shrewd rather than clairvoyant, like generic newspaper horoscopes designed for the credulous reader.

The gypsy probes a line. "You're a healer."

Meg, a speech pathologist, reminds herself that most women of her generation are in the so-called helping professions.

"You've weathered losses," the woman says, running her finger down a crease that arcs from thumb to wrist.

Did her parents' deaths within a year of each other mark her hand? The woman's statement requires no psychic gift: everyone loses.

"I see a long marriage," the fortune teller says. "Not an easy one."

Any woman Meg's age, wearing a wedding ring, has probably been married a while. And what marriage is easy?

The woman traces one of the lines that crisscross Meg's palm.

"Children. Two — but four pregnancies."

Meg swallows. How did she know that? Well, two children are average these days and who hasn't had a miss, or an abortion?

"Do you have any questions for me?" the woman asks.

"I'm thinking of leaving my husband," Meg whispers, embarrassed to half-believe in this stranger. "Can you see how that will turn out?"

The gypsy strokes the line down the middle of Meg's palm.

"The fate line," she says. "Some say the answer's here. I don't see it that way. It's all about choices and consequences."

Meg feels cheated. She wants a prediction, an oracle's pronouncement. This vague sybil knows more than she's saying: like the mammographer refusing to interpret the picture, holding off for the radiologist's higher authority. Come on, Meg always wants to say. Who are we kidding? You see hundreds of these every day. Just tell me.

The woman releases her hand.

"Thank you," says Meg, noticing with embarrassment a little basket baited with a five dollar bill, some ones. Aren't the hosts responsible, as for the magician or the pony handler at a birthday party? She'd leave a tip, but — like Jackie — has nothing in her evening bag except lipstick and comb. Walker will have to cover. *My husband's next,* she starts to say, by way of excuse, but holds back. Let the woman discern the relationship, if she's so clever.

"Tell your husband I'm ready," the gypsy says.

Walker has taken off his mask to talk with the economy on life support.

"You're on," she says.

Meg puts her gloves on, and lets Jackie's face dangle from her wrist by its elastic cord as she squeezes past the fortune teller's waiting customers. Pathetic, all these sophisticated party-goers in their clever costumes, all so eager. It's like the annual meetings with the retirement plan rep. Everyone wants a turn, even while debunking the young man in the borrowed office as a hired gun, wet behind the ears, purveyor of advice based on actuarial tables. No one puts too much faith in it, but you wouldn't want to waste the chance, just in case.

Wine and beer are on the granite counter by the deep sink — the kitchen's been done over since the last party. Meg pours a glass of red, ventures into the dining room and inspects the buffet. Only a giant punchbowl of candy corn, platters of limp vegetables and dry hummus,

46

and a few egg rolls congealed on a plate remain. Hesitating between a handful of the corn and an eggroll, she sips her wine.

"Looks like the plague of locusts got here first." The Pope without his miter, a red crease mark across his forehead, leans so close she smells citrus aftershave; her husband never wears anything like that. The man's very blond.

"How are you connected here?" he asks. His pale blue eyes beneath sand-white eyelashes stare for a beat too long before Meg replies.

"Sort of friends of friends," she says. "You?"

"I live in the neighborhood. Our kids went to school together."

He has a distinctive mouth. The bottom lip is full, the upper thin but with a graceful curve.

"It's a wonderful location," says Meg. "Must have been great for your kids, growing up down the street from the museums, the Library of Congress."

"I don't know," he says. "Parking's impossible. My house was burgled twice last year." *My house*, he says, not ours. Divorced or widowed? People their age are starting to die: she's fantasized that way out, Walker's death, or hers, if she's really mad.

"So who are you?" he asks.

Meg starts to introduce herself, then understands. "Jackie," she says, putting down her wine, slipping on her mask.

"Take it off," the Pope says. "You look like her anyway, you know."

Meg leaves the mask on. She imagines hearing him say it again, in the dimly lit, high-ceilinged bedroom of his townhouse around the corner: *Take it off, take it all off.* This electric tug of war, flirting with a stranger, probably happened to Jackie all the time.

Walker appears, in his mask.

"My husband," she says.

"Obviously. Jack, as a Catholic, I've always been a big fan. I'm enjoying chatting up your lovely wife."

"And you are?" Walker asks.

"Pope Benedict," he says and glides away in his red robe.

"She knew I was an engineer. She knew I was thinking about retiring. How does it work, do you think?"

"Educated guesses," says Meg. "And practice. Plus some kind of sixth sense."

"She said something's going to happen," he said. "To be ready."

Their host's teenage daughter jitters by in voluminous bell bottom pants, fringed vest, a campaign button: "Stay clean for Gene."

"It's time for the awards. Mom wants everyone in the living room."

"Awards?" asks Meg.

"We're giving out prizes! Everyone wins!" The girl shakes her long straight hair, lovely hippie, a blast of fresh air from the past.

Meg's feet hurt; she never wears heels. Wine on an empty stomach makes her head ache.

"Why don't we skip this," she says. "Let's go."

"But we're sure to win best in show," he says, over-confident as always.

"I just want to go home," she insists. The mask keeps her gaze forward; like blinders, it prevents looking for the Pope from the corner of her eye.

Clouds scud behind the Capitol dome and across the moon as they walk down the dark block in their masks. Her heels beat a harsh rhythm past the burnt out shell of the Eastern Market and a boarded-up school, graffiti spray painted across the brick walls. Walker beeps the car open as they approach the Saab.

She reaches out for her door. Something hard jabs between her ribs.

"Give me your bag, bitch," says a hoarse voice.

Maybe she would have seen him coming, if she hadn't been wearing the mask.

He dumps her lipstick and comb on the ground. "Where's your fucking money?"

"I've got whatever you want," says Walker from across the car roof.

"Any rings, cunt?" the boy says. He's young, she's sure even though she hasn't seen his face.

Meg holds out her left hand, trembling in the white glove.

"Take it off," the boy says.

She wrenches her rings over her knuckle.

"Don't hurt her. I've got money," Walker says.

"Take off that mask, bozo," the boy orders. "And put your keys, wallet, your phone, on the car."

Walker's ashen, slack-jawed with fear — vulnerable for once.

"What's the pin number for your card?" the boy demands.

Walker recites their wedding date: 7-4-78. She's surprised; it's her password, too, though she's never told him. They've kept separate accounts, except for the house, tuitions.

The gun's muzzle withdraws. She breathes and discovers an aching bruise. The boy appears on the far side of the car; he is even younger than she'd guessed. He puts Walker's mask on. Incongruous dreadlocks sprout from Kennedy's plastic pompadour.

"Who's this dude, anyway?" he asks.

"Kennedy," says Walker. "JFK."

"Step back from the car," the boy says.

Meg balances on the curb; Walker stands in the middle of the street. The car squeals away.

She knows what's going to happen the instant before it does. Meg's turned fortune teller now: reading tomorrow's headline in the Metro section, seeing the photograph of herself, her Jackie self, in a blood-stained pink suit, grieving Pieta-style over her fallen husband.

Just as she's foreseen, the boy makes a u-turn and drives back — straight toward Walker, stranded in the middle of the street.

Then the Saab swerves to miss him and the sound is back-fire not gunshot. The boy laughs out the window, his game of chicken over; the car roars away. Walker stumbles across the street. She should run to embrace him but remains rooted to the curb.

He'd almost drowned on their honeymoon, pulled by a riptide out from the Jamaican beach. A native man plunged into the surf and pulled him in, then waited for a tip while they kissed on the sand, the deep kiss of relief and reprieve. It all could have ended so early.

And now here they are, reprieved again. Cast up on the concrete beach of the curb, alive. It must be shock that's making her so numb, so cold.

"That was close," he says. "Let's go call the police."

She follows him back to the party, still wearing her mask.

Entangled Objects

Meg cracked open the new package of extra-sheer control-top pantyhose: Christmas Eve on the town, something different for this, their first without children or parents. This simpler, pared down holiday would be easier with no one but themselves to please.

Think of it as freedom, release from booby-trapped traditions, she admonished herself. Think of it as a consolation prize for the empty nest. Holiday gatherings had sparked some memorable fights between Meg and Walker, fueled by complicated, combustible expectations and obligations. A Christmas fight had become almost a tradition. Overall, she and Walker argued less these days — fortunately, since making up came harder now with sex less reliable. But at times like tonight she almost missed the heat of the fray. Oh well, it would be good for them, going out for a romantic evening. Living well is the best revenge, as the Spanish say.

The phone rang. In the midst of pulling on her stockings, Meg let the machine answer. Superstitious, she believed not running to answer increased the odds of a call from a far-flung girl in another time zone: one daughter wandering, volunteering on an organic farm in Italy, the other an exchange student in Japan. Yearning for their voices was like the remembered ache of being young and waiting for a lover's call.

"Hi, Susan August here. I e-mailed the comparables to you at work, Walker. But since you may not be in the office over Christmas, what's your home e-mail?"

A local institution, Susan was the realtor who'd sold them the house twenty years ago, touting it as a wonderful family home, albeit a fixer-upper, a handy man special. She explained the place was originally built as a summer cottage, without even upstairs plumbing. "It's been re-modeled and re-muddled quite a bit since then," she'd said.

Walker hadn't mentioned contacting Susan, but he had been brooding over their recent reassessment and the increase in property taxes. According to the couple's long-standing division of labor, he carried the burden of worry about money and she worried about health.

But Walker took everything too seriously. There was nothing new or urgent about their finances or the eighty-year old house; they could remain for the duration — or at least the foreseeable future. Way too soon to be serious about downsizing, and certainly not the market for selling.

Meg pulled the cleaner's film off her black dress. Tonight the walk-in closet felt like a refrigerator. Their rambling bungalow exemplified energy inefficiency. Drafty as a sieve — a fault that likely saved their lives the night the furnace malfunctioned. Shivering, Meg fantasized for a moment about a sleek, warm condo downtown with double-glazed windows and glittering views. Maybe it was time to downsize. She dismissed the disloyal thought. They'd raised the girls here; their family history had seeped into the plaster walls. You love your house and depend on it, despite its imperfections. Like a spouse.

She stepped into the bathroom to do her makeup, enjoying the recently regained convenience of running water upstairs. Last summer the ancient galvanized pipes leading to the second floor sprang leaks and Walker turned the upstairs water off as a temporary fix. The plumber recommended copper pipes. Walker procrastinated, deferring decision, expense, and upheaval. With only the two of them, they could manage with just the bathroom downstairs, for awhile, he said. Meg grew increasingly irritated with the hike downstairs to the bathroom as weeks dragged into months. Two weeks ago, suddenly, Walker summoned the plumber to finish the job. Wonderful having the upstairs bathrooms back — even if they remained small and old-fashioned.

Meg applied the finishing touch of mascara, lipstick. The light above the medicine cabinet buzzed. If they ever did sell this house it would still be a fixer-upper, despite all their work.

Not long after they moved in, a woman stopped by on a nostalgia trip, having lived in the house as a child. Meg walked her through; the woman said it had been her mother who first put plumbing in upstairs, squeezing the two small adjoining bathrooms under the eaves. The visitor seemed reluctant to leave and lingered on the porch. "We moved here from Boston to be near my father," she revealed. "He was a patient at the Lodge." Meg told her the Lodge was closed now, the former psychiatric hospital slated for re-development as condos.

"We had some happy times here, and sad ones," the woman said, before she finally drove away.

For a while after that visitor, odd features of the upstairs bathrooms troubled Meg. Why did one bathroom door lock only from the exterior? What was the purpose of the tiny window — a swinging shutter with a glass knob — between the bathrooms? Had the locked bath served as an isolation cell for the psychiatric patient home on a weekend pass? Did his wife design the window for observation?

She pestered Walker with her questions and theories until he promised to cover the peek-hole with sheetrock and to remove the exterior lock on the door. But these tasks merited low priority on his endless list of maintenance and repair. Over time, she stopped noticing the lock. And when the girls became teenagers and commandeered both bathrooms to shower simultaneously, the peek-hole proved handy for sharing shampoo and conditioner.

Everything circled back to her absent daughters tonight. She opened the closed door of their room. Ridiculous to keep it like some sort of museum to their childhood: time to re-decorate. The deserted room felt forlorn and cold — the radiator off, a conservation measure.

Meg sat at their too-tidy dressing table and blasted the warm breath of a left-behind hair dryer, sprayed herself from a sample-size atomizer of *Happy*. Let it be so, she thought. And then felt ridiculous, an aging imposter in the cheerful citrus scent. She should have used her own special occasion Chanel, Walker's gift from the duty free in Charles de Gaulle, at her suggestion. You learn to coach and coax for what you want.

She put on her black pumps, her highest heels. Her party shoes, the girls teased.

Meg buttoned her black wool coat. Reconsidered, and defiantly exchanged it for her mother's vintage Persian lamb. Her vegetarian daughters disapproved of the fur; tonight she'd be elegant and warm, and protest their absence.

The heavy coat felt cumbersome and her feet hurt in unaccustomed heels as she walked to the Metro. She rode the train to the Friendship Heights station and hailed a cab.

"Georgetown, Blues Alley on Wisconsin." Just saying the words, naming the destination, elevated her spirits. Such a good idea, she congratulated herself, getting Walker these tickets to hear his favorite singer live, for the first time. A treat for both of them, instead of giving him another merino vest for moths to eat.

Outside the club, the line snaked along the sidewalk. Perennially prompt, Walker waited near the front of the queue — tall and dapper in dark topcoat, briefcase tucked under his arm.

"Your mother's coat?"

After thirty years, you read the other's mind. Spooky action, she called the phenomena, after the principle of responsive connections between entangled objects, learned in a long-ago physics course. Disappointed, she translated his invisible subtitles. *You look dowdy.*

Checking the offending coat revealed his favorite dress. The forgiving velvet fit well despite the irritating extra pounds that had crept up on her since turning fifty. He kissed her, approving — then sniffed.

"What's that perfume?"

She'd hurt his feelings, not using the Chanel. "Just something I found, hurrying, at the last minute." Her chronic tardiness, her belief in the elasticity of time had once been such a bone of contention. By now she accepted he liked to be early, and he knew she always ran late. Simply one of the minor irreconcilable differences woven into the fabric of their marriage: warp and weft, yin and yang.

The dark, low-ceilinged club felt like a warm cave. The hostess seated them at one of the tiny tables squeezed in tight as eggs in a crate. Meg read the menu with the appreciation of a ten-day dieter about to fall off the wagon. Everything was rich, delicious, and forbidden. Tonight — enjoy! Plenty of time after the holidays to be strict.

A skinny waitress, kohl smeared around her eyes like a goth raccoon, arrived. "What will it be?"

"French onion soup, the steak au poivre," said Meg.

"Rice or French fries?"

"Pommes frites," she said, trying to catch Walker's eye. They used to speak French over the girls' heads — their secret language.

Wearing newly necessary reading glasses, Walker perused the thick wine list. He'd always prided himself on his twenty-twenty vision. The glasses signaled future vulnerabilities. How would the two of them stand up to the tests of age? Meg touched his hand.

"Doesn't this remind you, of our bistro on the Ile?"

They'd celebrated her fiftieth birthday in Paris; staying in a flat on the Ile St. Louis, eating so often at the neighborhood place on the corner Meg pretended they belonged.

Applause greeted the singer stepping into the spotlight. Swathed in expensive bohemian-chic layers, she looked smaller and younger than in photographs. The fragile waif look, Meg thought — envious.

The singer introduced her band: percussion, keyboard, and sax. Her voice when she began to sing was no waif's but all sultry torch.

I've got a crush on you, the chanteuse crooned. She and the saxophonist traded solo riffs with seamless rapport. They'd been married; now divorced they still worked and traveled together. How difficult that must be.

But, Meg thought, difficulty is at the heart of any partnership. And marriage operated the way Walker explained the stock market: you must expect peaks and valleys on the graph, hang in for the long run. You fall in and out of love, over the years. She touched Walker's hand again. He listened to the music, oblivious.

Meg lifted her soup spoon, trailing filaments of melted cheese. Delicious.

She felt gratified, even smug, to have chosen such a perfect gift for him, for them both. Tonight represented a victory after an annus horribilis: youngest daughter floundering in and out of college, investments melting like sugar in coffee, his father's death.

The singer chose *Violets for my Furs* as her encore, as though she knew it was Walker's favorite; Meg felt like claiming credit.

She broke the crust on her crème brulée, so creamy and sweet it melted on her tongue. Perfectly balanced, like the counterpoise of liquid gold sax and tinsel-bright drums.

"A bite of this for one of your mousse?"

He shook his head, pushing his ramekin toward her.

Meg polished off both desserts.

While Walker retrieved their coats, Meg queued for the new CD. Especially since the girls were gone she loved to fill the empty house with music — discs, radio, even their old records from college. One night, while he was brushing his teeth, she put The Doors on the turntable and waited naked for him in bed. The music, with the whispering extra resonance from vinyl, played like an aphrodisiac sound track from another life. For the first time in ages, she'd felt wild and enjoyed making noise. Why not? No babies to wake, no night-crawling teenagers to embarrass.

Meg's turn arrived to have her CD autographed.

"Who is this for?" the singer asked. At close range, her piquant face looked pale with fatigue. She still had a second show to sing.

"To Walker, please. My husband's a huge fan."

The singer scrawled her silver signature across the jewel case, adding: *To Walker with Love.*

What did the singer mean? Did she really love her audience?

Meg, a speech therapist, sometimes felt affection for a client — a maternal impulse, inspired by the client's need and effort. But something far different generated between a good singer and audience. Passion, not caritas, was expected and sanctioned.

Later, she would point out the inscription to Walker; tease him for being such a groupie.

Her shoes pinched as she walked to his car.

"Wasn't she wonderful?" She fastened her seatbelt, slipped off the shoes, and wiggled her toes. Blessed relief! Meg stretched and leaned back, relaxed and fuzzy from wine and food and music. "You never really know, how a star's going to be, in person, do you? Mary Travers — what a disaster." Even after more than thirty years, Meg recalled the wretched disappointment of that show at Passim's in Harvard

Square: the star's mechanical performance and ossified face, the stiff fringe of bleached blond hair. The singer had seemed to impersonate herself; looked half-dead. And now, she was all dead. Having the idols of her youth gone made Meg feel old.

Walker drove without comment.

And she realized her mistake, the reason for his stony silence.

He hadn't been with her at Passim's, though he loved Peter, Paul and Mary. Meg had purchased the tickets as a peace offering after one of their fights senior year in college. They'd been on a roller coaster of breaking up and reconciliation — afraid of the future bearing down with graduation.

What had provoked that next fight, the night before the show? She could not remember. Meg almost tore up the expensive tickets, but then she had invited their friend Seth instead. Afterward, stoned and still angry, she slept with Seth (handsome, as casual about sex as Walker was serious).

Ashamed and remorseful, she confessed to Walker. They broke up and did not reconcile. Commencement came and they went their separate ways. She threw herself into a long distance relationship with Seth, which ultimately proved foolish.

Five years later Meg and Walker re-encountered each other at a friend's birthday party. It was love at second sight, Meg liked to say. They courted briefly and eloped — desperate to make sure of each other before anything else could happen.

But from time to time over the first years of their marriage, something triggered him. They would be making love and the wound would open, and he would question her about Seth. Did you do this with him? What did he do? How did you like it? She learned to leave the bed and let the outbreak run its course, like a fever. After the children came, the flare-ups diminished and finally ceased, as though the hurt had burned out. Or perhaps they had grown into a deeper security, even if it entailed taking each other for granted. Or they had grown tired. They still fought, of course, but never about Seth. The incident faded like a bad dream.

In the too-quiet car, she played the new CD. The romantic music grated like finger nails on slate and she ejected the disc.

They arrived home to a cold, dark house.

"Let's make a fire," she suggested.

"It's late," he said.

"Only eleven. We still have the tree to decorate."

He might refuse, go upstairs; leave the evening ruined.

"I'll bring in some wood," he said.

Isn't it good, Norwegian wood, she thought, tempted to put the album on but afraid to evoke more dangerous memories. Turning on the radio, she fiddled with the tuning until she found an ethereal, sexless boys' choir singing Benjamin Britten's *Ceremony of Carols*.

Meg pulled a sweatshirt over her dress and located her slippers beneath the kitchen table, waiting there since breakfast. She carried liqueur a client had given her into the living room. Soon the fire would take the chill off the room, and a drink would warm them.

"Drambuie—unsolicited gift from my client. Worth breaking the ethics code," she said, and cringed at the brittle brightness in her voice. What a time to mention ethics.

Walker knelt untangling the lights. He plugged in a string to test it. "Lots of duds."

"I'll get new ones, at the sales after Christmas," she said, the promise made and broken every year. She avoided the stores and their tawdry leftover holiday merchandise in January.

"Sip?" Meg held out her glass.

He shook his head, dismissing the offer — the way he refused the bite of crème brulée on her spoon. She felt a jab of irritation. Unnecessary for him to be so abstemious; he didn't weigh any more now than the day they were married. He had a taste for martyrdom.

Strand by strand, Walker draped the branches with lights. The dark tree shimmered to life.

"Maybe we should skip ornaments and just have lights," she said, remembering their first sparsely decorated tree.

Meg set to work. Tree-trimming with the girls, after he did the lights, was her job. Except for the star — they needed his height for that.

The ornament box held a time capsule of all the years: macaroni angels, bright tin birds from Mexico, gilded pine cones, the lopsided star fashioned from tongue depressors spangled with glue and glitter.

Walker poked the fire, added a log, and leaned against the mantle. She hung her grandmother's fragile glass icicles.

"Ready for the star," she said.

Walker's lips twitched — a signal that he was about to say something important, or hold it back.

"Penny for your thoughts," she said, holding out the star.

His fierce expression startled her. Suddenly, he resembled his father at the very end: stern features drawn taut with pain. "I've been thinking of leaving."

Meg felt as if she'd neglected to check her rearview mirror and totaled the car pulling out of her own driveway, overconfident on a familiar stretch of road.

He'd fixed the plumbing. He'd called the realtor for comparables. Elephants mate for life, and have two languages. One audible, another one infrasonic rumbles, detected only through a change in air pressure. She should have known.

The tree blinked idiot warning lights, illuminating a litter of tissue paper and Styrofoam pellets from the ornament box scattered across the glossy hardwood floor. Fifteen years ago they'd worked together to prepare the floors for refinishing. Crawled together on hands and knees like penitents; pulling out old carpet staples.

He walked out of the room, up the stairs.

Don't pursue him, she told herself. Let him go. Wait it out.

The shower roared. He never showered at night. She recognized the tactic; taught it to him. Besieged by crying babies, craving respite, she used to shut herself in the bathroom alone and run the shower at deafening full blast.

The shock ebbed; anger flooded every vein.

How dare he spring this now? How dare he leave? Now after forgiving her all these years? After all she'd forgiven him?

Meg stamped upstairs and flipped the exterior lock on the bathroom door. He was a danger to himself and others — to her, the girls. She would make him prisoner and keep him safe, as that other woman had done with another lunatic husband in this house years ago.

The water stopped. She tiptoed into the other bathroom next door and opened the peek-hole. He leaned away from her, stretched down to towel his feet. His body was still beautiful — long torso, so slender she could see his ribs.

He twisted the doorknob and discovered his captivity.

"Meg! Let me out!" Yelling, believing her downstairs.

"Is there someone else?" she said, through the open peek-hole. Certain there was not. He was fiercely, protectively monogamous. That much she knew. Almost knew.

"No," he said.

"Why now?"

"It's enough," he said. "All these years and you're still thinking about him."

"I wasn't. I mentioned Mary Travers, that's all. *You* thought about him."

"So what happened that night was so unimportant, you forgot."

"If it mattered so much we should never have gotten married."

"That can be fixed." He slammed the door to the porthole, closing the chink in the wall between them. "Let me out. This is crazy."

She flung the shutter open. "You're the crazy one. Digging up ancient history! Talking about divorce, out of the clear blue!"

A trapped animal glared back at her. "Not exactly the clear blue."

The phone rang — the midnight bell demanding answer. She ran.

"Merry Christmas!" Libby in Japan, voice clear as though calling from the carport, home right at curfew time. "It's been Christmas day here for hours already. I thought you guys might still be up, decorating the tree."

"Dad's gone to bed," she lied. From a million miles away their grown child had once more sensed the danger, overheard and interrupted. Libby had always hated it, when they fought.

She pressed the cordless to her ear and walked past the silence of the bathroom door, listening to Libby all the way downstairs. Listening as she stood beside the tree, breathing the resinous forest scent. Listening and missing her daughter, missing everyone who had ever left her.

"Well, I should say sayonara. Tell Dad I love him, and Merry Christmas!"

Loneliness squeezed her heart like a vise. And shame — she should have shared; passed the phone to Walker in his cell. If he left, what would they tell the children?

We're both crazy, she thought. The residue of that other mad man and his family's suffering had infected them, exacerbated their own pain and failings. Spores of sadness lurking in this house were breaking through now the girls were gone. Poisoning them insidiously, like lethal flakes of lead paint.

Meg unwrapped the Christmas stockings from layers of protective tissue; inhaled the bitter scent of mothballs. What did frankincense smell like? She felt a lump in the toe of her stocking, reached in, and drew out a pewter charm. The couple traded it back and forth each year. "Meet me under the mistletoe," the engraving read.

Holding the coin in her fist like a charm against evil, she mounted the stairs.

She would release him. Let him march past her in plaid pajama armor and down the stairs to his study. Ignore the clang of the sleeper couch opening. And if he made good on his threat and left in the morning, she would ignore the final thud of the front door closing. Let this be the weary end: the final fight, the ultimate unforgivable petty injury.

Meg crept down the hallway past the locked door and into the other bathroom. She opened the little window.

He stared at her, bleak eyes veined red.

She produced the pewter charm, rubbing it between thumb and forefinger, holding it just out of his reach. Like a magician preparing to make it disappear, or to pull it out of thin air, from behind his ear.

Meg extended her hand, holding the charm flat on her palm: the way the riding teacher taught the girls to offer sugar to a horse. So the teeth can't hurt you.

"I found this in my stocking. Has the offer expired?"

She held out her invitation to continue their ridiculous Mummers dance of love. Like cartoon violence — blow it up, punch it down, watch it spring back to life.

Meg offered the charm; not as an olive branch but in an opening bid for reparation.

Chinese Vermilion

Silver Mylar pillows float on jets of air in my favorite room of the Andy Warhol Museum in Pittsburgh. Walking through is like swimming underwater among a school of silver fish. My cell phone buzzed there during the Bar Association's cocktail reception.

"You're late. Sounds like a party," said my thirteen year old daughter Zoe, accusingly.

Since my husband Charlie and I split up a year earlier, she always needed to know my whereabouts.

"A work thing. I'm leaving now. Be there soon," I said.

The connection was bad, the signal obscured by the brick walls of the old factory which houses the museum. Outside, walking to the car, I called back.

"I need a display board for my science project. It's due tomorrow," Zoe announced.

"Why didn't you tell me before?"

"I was at Dad's." She plays that card all the time; we shouldn't let her.

Zoe's not doing well in school, or anywhere else. An adjustment reaction, the therapist, Dr. Steiner, says. Normal regression that time will help, along with structure, and routine. But our train wreck requires her to alternate between two houses and cope with her dad's new wife and baby. I let Charlie have the house; it worked out better financially and I imagined making a fresh start. Our old house — his house — is walking distance from Zoe's school. So I pick her up there, my weeks. Though I tell her to have her backpack by the door so I can just summon her from the car, she's never ready. I must wait in the foyer, an outsider in my own house. If Charlie's home, we make conversation, confirm calendars. Whether he's there or not, I'm always aware of Sylvia and the baby. Invisible, somewhere upstairs. She hides the baby as though I'm the bad fairy, the one with the evil eye.

I slid into my car — silver, with leather upholstery, a consolation prize to myself — and started toward the tunnel. Just before entering the silent zone under the river, my phone rang again.

"Zoe, I'm on my way."

"It's me," said Charlie. "She just told me about this science thing. I'm sorry. I asked before."

"You've got to check the teachers' websites like Dr. Steiner said."

"I know. You're right."

Zoe let me in, then disappeared upstairs for her stuff. I picked up my mail from the gate-leg table — my table, a piece from my grandmother's house. Charlie's keeping things I don't have room for, protecting Zoe from ripping apart the familiar rooms completely. Opening my high school magazine, making a mental note to send Clear Spring Friends a change of address, I turned to the Alumni Notes section:

In Memoriam, Ben Markham, Class of '69, at his home in Venice, California, after a long illness.

Ben was a soccer star, a minor god, a senior when I was an obscure freshman. He would never have noticed me except I was the only member of my class to have a small speaking part in the fall play — Antigone's sister. After the performance, Ben burst into the girls' dressing room, bounded to Antigone, and swept her back in a deep kiss.

"Out of here, Ben," the drama teacher ordered.

He sauntered past. I held the bed-sheet toga against my bare chest.

"You were beautiful," he said and gave me a quick kiss. My mouth stung with surprise.

"Out, Ben! Now!" said the teacher.

He dropped a sarcastic bow and left. I dipped a tissue in the cold cream and erased my makeup, leaving the lipstick on.

That fall I attended every soccer game, shivering in the deepening autumn chill, watching Ben flash up the field, the tendons behind his knees pulling and straining as he kicked the ball. Between classes, my heart thudded when I glimpsed his narrow-hipped frame in the crowded hall. Once or twice he smiled at me. In the student lounge, I checked my mailbox, hoping he might leave a note. But instead my friend (beautiful as Snow White with fair skin and dark hair) received his sketches, invitations to walk in the woods. She returned from those walks with pine needles in her hair.

When he dropped her, we freshman girls closed ranks, sitting with her at lunch and talking louder when he passed, his arm looped around Antigone. That spring he was almost kicked out for drugs; the soccer coach and the art teacher saved him. It helped with the Disciplinary Committee that his father had just died.

"Hey, April." Charlie leaned against the newel post at the foot of the stairs, surprising me with his quiet approach in stocking feet. The brown merino cardigan (my gift to him our last Christmas together) had baby spit-up on the shoulder. He looked tired but content.

Dazed by the news about Ben, I had to share it. "Someone from Clear Spring died."

"A teacher?"

"No, a guy a couple years ahead of me."

"Makes you feel old, doesn't it, when we start showing up in the obituary page."

"We're old enough. Even if you have a brand-new life."

"April, please," he said. Meaning not here, not now. Not where Zoe might hear, not with Sylvia eavesdropping while she nursed her baby in some corner of my house.

"Zoe, let's get a move on," I yelled up the staircase.

We parked at the strip mall, between Pearl Arts and Crafts and the Chinese place. "Here," I said, opening my wallet — which I do too often with Zoe. "Go get the display board and I'll pick up dinner."

"You never get what I like. You get the board, I'll go to the China Garden," she said.

Dr. Steiner says set limits, insist on respect. At the end of a long day I'm not always up to it. I handed over thirty dollars.

Fluorescent lights illuminated Pearl's jumble of inkpads, rubber stamps, glue guns, picture frames, diaries and note cards. Hurrying, I turned a corner and came upon a rack of silver tubes of paint. For a moment, despite the dry air of the suburban store, I breathed a ghost scent: turpentine and oil from Pearl Paint on Canal Street in Manhattan, visited only once, twenty-five years earlier, with Ben.

Now I saw the remembered brand: *Holbein Artists' Oil Colors, The World's Finest.* I scanned the labels: *Aureolin, Cerulean Blue, Geranium Lake, Mars Orange.* And *Chinese Vermilion*: "List price $52.80, Pearl Price $39.60." How much had it cost in 1976? I only recalled my surprise that paint could be so valuable.

"That's the good stuff," Ben had said. "Out of my price range."

Ben graduated from Friends in 1969, in red velvet bell-bottoms, defying the dress code. He disappeared, not the sort of alum to return to the quiet campus. Three years later, I wore the requisite white dress to my own commencement ceremony in the Meeting House. After four more years, I graduated from Mount Holyoke and moved to Manhattan.

I lived with a girl named Nina; the college vocational office matched us. Assigned cabin mates; our relationship fell somewhere between friendship and business. In our tiny apartment kitchen, you could not have the refrigerator and the silverware drawer open simultaneously. The living-room ceiling was high, though, with two comfortable chairs for reading in front of the bricked-in fireplace. A card table and folding chairs comprised the dining area. The only window overlooked an airshaft; we craned our necks to see the sky and guess the weather. We shared a windowless bedroom and a bathroom with black-and-white tile in basket weave.

The building — a converted hotel, once popular with musicians playing Carnegie Hall around the corner — had a doorman, a comfort to my parents three hundred miles away in Virginia. Next door was a Hungarian restaurant with a violinist. We couldn't afford to eat out often, or go to concerts; Nina worked for a publisher and I was a paralegal. But many nights we attended the continuous film festival in Carnegie Hall's basement theater. The cramped black-box cinema has vanished now, with its lobby café where I drank my first espresso, loving the bitter taste, the heavy white demitasse cups.

One January evening just after dinner, the phone rang. Nina, quick on slim bare feet, ran to answer.

"Your mother," she said. We usually talked Saturdays, when the rates were down. It was odd for her to call mid-week.

"Hi, dear," she said. "Someone called, Ben Markham. From Friends. He thinks he saw you last night, at a movie. I gave him your number."

So she delivered the hoped-for message, eight years late.

"Time to go," said Nina. "If you want coffee before the movie."

"I'll just stay in and read."

"And miss *Jules and Jim*?"

"I'm tired," I said, with a twinge of disloyalty — to Nina, sisterhood, our shared subscription to *Ms.* magazine.

"All right," she said in the tone familiar from when I dated a summer associate until the bland courtship fizzled after a few dinners, Shakespeare in the Park.

She left. After rifling the pages of the phonebook for Ben without success, I poured a tumbler from the scotch reserved for Nina's father's visits from Connecticut; it landed like an ember in my stomach.

The phone rang.

"Is this April?" A midnight disk jockey voice.

"Yes."

"Ben Markham, from Clear Spring. Think I saw you last night at the Carnegie."

"I live in the neighborhood."

We talked until he suggested continuing in person. "I'll take you out for coffee. See you in half an hour."

Sometimes I borrowed Nina's clothes, but that night I opted for my own jeans, a sweater, and my blue boots — artificial leather, bright as a Crayola. I did use Nina's lipstick from Bergdorf's, creamier than my drugstore stuff, and lined my eyes with kohl. Brushing my short hair, I hoped to look like Fellini's star, like a blond Giulietta Masina. Upon moving to New York, I'd sacrificed my long hair, offering it up in exchange for glamour, spending a shocking amount of my first paycheck.

The intercom buzzed.

"A Mr. Markham's here," said the doorman.

"Send him up."

He looked older, in a camelhair coat a touch too loose, a crimson scarf around his neck.

"For you," he said, holding out a long-stemmed red rose.

"Thank you." Thorns pricked through the green florist tissue. Nina said you knew you'd left Mount Holyoke when trees stopped wearing nametags and roses had thorns. I filled a glass with water and put the flower on the mantel above our extinct fireplace, careful as though on stage, conscious of him watching.

"You like portraits," he said, looking at the gallery above the mantle. We had lavished one whole Sunday on the project — choosing our favorites from the gift shop at the Met, taping them up, arranging and re-arranging, laughing and drinking a bottle of Frascati. Suddenly I was ashamed of the old-fashioned pictures.

A friend from high school turned up, I scribbled on the pad by the phone. *Gone for coffee.*

The elevator was hothouse sweet from the stiff eucalyptus in a wall sconce. He stroked my jacket — silvery, feathery fake fur. "Great coat," he said.

"Good night, miss," said the doorman, touching his cap. I swept by, imperious as though I had gentleman callers every evening.

"Let's go to Rumplemeyer's. Special occasion, after all," he said.

Rumplemeyer's was warm as a conservatory. Our table by the window overlooked the dark park across the avenue.

"I saw Liz Taylor in here once," Ben said.

"She ate with Richard Burton at an Italian place, where I went to college, when they were filming *Who's Afraid of Virginia Woolf.*"

"Where'd you go?"

"Holyoke," I said. "You went to art school, right?"

"For a while. In Paris. Now I'm taking classes at the Art Students League. I pay the rent with advertising gigs — logos."

I didn't know what logo meant but did not ask.

Ben ordered cocoa for two. "The whipped cream is outrageous here," he told me when the waiter brought huge cups topped with clouds of cream. The jacket photograph on the Tijuana Brass album flashed into my mind — a naked girl buried in froth.

Afterward, we strolled down the sidewalk, skirting piles of dirty snow in the cold night air. Carriages waited by the empty fountain at the Plaza; the blanketed horses shivered.

"I'll take you on a ride around the park," Ben said. "When I get paid." He tucked my hand in his coat pocket; the satin lining grew warm.

"I'd like to come up," he said as we stood beneath the striped awning over my building's door.

"My roommate's home," I said — resenting Nina, waiting upstairs.

"How about dinner tomorrow? After I deliver some work downtown, we could eat in the Village. Meet me at Pearl Paint, on Canal."

He kissed me good night, beneath the taxi light and the doorman's stare.

The elevator mirror reflected my flushed face: desire pumping beneath my skin, obvious as the veins and organs in that transparent plastic toy, The Visible Woman.

Nina looked up from her book. "You missed a good one. But tomorrow's *Shoot the Piano Player*."

"Actually, I'm going out."

She sniffed, as if scenting the whipped cream and kiss on my breath. "That's a pretty rose. I didn't know anyone from your high school was up here."

I retreated to the bathroom, shutting the door though usually we left it open, and took a long shower, fogging the mirror.

The next day I fidgeted over my task: a tedious document search, reading reams of telexes for key names and dates. At lunch, I sneaked into the corner office of the partner emeritus who never came to work. Sitting in his leather desk chair, swiveling back and forth, I gazed out the plate glass window as fat flakes of snow sifted down over the stalled traffic on Park Avenue.

Finally, 5:30 came. I freshened my eyeliner and lipstick, and rode the subway downtown to an unfamiliar neighborhood of hardware stores and plastic wholesalers behind cast-iron storefronts with columns and flourishes like piped icing. I found Pearl Paint; Ben waited just inside the door.

"Catholic school girl look today, except for those boots," he said, smiling at my work uniform of straight skirt, turtleneck, navy duffel coat with big patch pockets.

He grabbed my hand and towed me between the towering shelves and labyrinthine aisles to the paints: *Holbein Artists' Oil Colors, The World's Finest.*

"That's the good stuff," he said. "Out of my price range." He pinned me against the shelf of paints, thrusting his hands deep inside my pockets and massaging my thighs. We kissed until he blew on my eyelids.

"Open. I want to match your eyes." Ben juggled paint tubes. "Cobalt Blue? Hydrangea?"

"Can I help you?" asked a young black-clad clerk.

"What color are her eyes? Oh, perfect. Verditer Blue."

The clerk grinned and left.

"Can I help you?" Ben whispered, his lips against my earlobe. "Let's go home for dinner."

He hustled me past the cash registers and outside into the blistering cold. I dug my hands into my pockets and discovered something hard and smooth: cached paint tubes. Frightened, I looked over my shoulder, half-expecting pursuit by an angry clerk.

Ben pressed his fingers to my lips. "The markup is insane," he said. "Don't be mad."

Now my cell phone rang, insistent.

"There's a coupon. We can have eggrolls or extra pancakes for the Moo Shu," said Zoe.

"Which ever you want is fine."

"Are you sure about the eggrolls? Last time you said they were too greasy."

"Zoe, you can make a simple decision without me."

"Well, excuse me. Just trying to be more considerate, like you and Dad are always saying."

I snapped the phone closed; I couldn't stop staring at the rack of paints.

On the train uptown, Ben held the strap with one arm and me with the other, cushioning the jolts. At 79th Street we climbed cracked concrete stairs. His building was a shabby nineteenth-century dinosaur; on the stoop, two men sat drinking from a paper bag. He ushered me four flights up, then inside, snapping the deadbolt, shoving another bolt across the door, hooking a chain.

"Excuse the mess," he said, hanging my coat on a hook by the door. I felt a complicit guilt as he emptied my pockets of half a dozen paints. He tossed the paints onto a heavy oak sideboard, laden with brushes and rags, beneath an expanse of bare window, beside a covered easel.

The cavernous, one-room apartment smelled of turpentine. Stove, sink, and refrigerator lined the back wall; a massive library table claimed the center of the floor. Bookshelves covered one wall and paintings layered another — real paintings in frames, oils and watercolors. A mattress with blood red sheets, a magnetic pool of color, filled the far corner.

"Sit," Ben said, pulling a stool out from under the table. He opened a bottle of wine. "We'll let it breathe. It's worth waiting." His knife flickered along flat green leaves which released a pungent scent.

"What's that?"

"Cilantro. Secret Vietnamese weapon discovered in Paris." He pushed it into a neat heap, like grass cuttings. "You could chop the scallions."

I hacked the stems.

"No. Like this." He covered my hand and made the knife dance. Soon red oil sizzled in a deep wok; the pot of water came to a boil. "Almost there. Rice noodles cook fast," he said.

In his bathroom, traffic noise and cold air seeped in around the edges of the window. Postcards and antique photographs of Paris papered the walls. The medicine cabinet's pressed glass knob tempted me. Inside were dental floss, shaving cream, and a prescription bottle: Valium, prescribed for Sandy Johnson. Who was she? What claim did she have to Ben's bathroom?

"Ready!" he called.

Candlelight fell on a mound of translucent noodles gleaming on a white platter, drizzled with red sauce and a garnish of cilantro. I'd never had a man cook for me before.

"To chance encounters," he said, raising a crystal wineglass, its thick stem cut like a prism.

For dessert, he offered a bowl of tangerines and jasmine tea from a white porcelain pot. Blossoms floated in the pale liquid — too sweet for me, like drinking perfume. Ben peeled a tangerine and arranged it on a plate like a flower, then fed it to me, petal by petal.

Afterward, he pushed the dishes aside. "Come, I'll show you something."

On the sideboard a tiny oil painting, no bigger than a playing card, stood on a plate stand. Rich daubs of color — smoke and black, touches of red — conjured a winter street scene of rusty snow and carriages.

"An original Robert Henri. One of his *pochades,* a pocket picture. My grandfather collected his work. Dad pissed most of it away, and Mom had to auction the leftovers. I helped myself to this one."

Ben picked up a stack of little pictures and fanned them out on the buffet, like a hand of cards. "I painted these. My *pochades.*"

In one, a dash of red paint indicated a figure beside the Plaza fountain; in another, a stream of yellow taxis swirled around Columbus Circle.

"I'm working on this now," he said, uncovering the easel to reveal a large oil of a nude with shadow black hair, dusky skin, crimson nipples and lips. Sandy Johnson.

"Beautiful," I said. Facing him, I pulled my sweater off, stepped out of my skirt and trembled in tights and bra, my blue boots.

"Turn around," he said. "I'll help."

As he unhooked my bra, sparks cascaded down my spine.

He picked up a tube of the stolen paint. "Chinese Vermilion," he said, his delicate fingers unscrewing the cap. "Nothing like red for accent." He dabbed it on my nipples and pressed his paint-smeared finger to my lips. It tasted bitter. "Lead paint is poisonous," he whispered, then sucked my nipples.

Ben carried me to the crimson mattress. Kneeling above me, he unzipped my boots, peeled down my tights, eased off my panties.

"Let's see how you are with zippers," he said, guiding my hand to his fly. Soon he was naked, doing what I wanted. Later, he did something new, which hurt, but I wanted that, too.

He fell asleep. Car lights from the street below swept across the ceiling; horns honked. It seemed like trying to rest on a traffic island but I curled against his warm back and finally slept.

Later, someone pounded on the door, yelling: "Let me in! Open the goddamn door!"

Ben tensed. "Shh," he breathed. "My neighbor, too much to drink."

The man kept banging on the door. Ben wrapped his arms around me. When the noise stopped, we made love and drifted to sleep. Then the phone began to ring. It rang and rang until Ben took it off the hook.

In the morning, light flooded the apartment. Ben stood at the easel, working on Sandy's portrait.

"Shower?" he asked. "The faucet's broken, you'll have to use the pliers."

77

"No, thanks." I wanted a hot bath in my own clean tub, and fresh clothes.

"I'll take you to breakfast."

The diner across the street was small and steamy, crowded with workmen, hardhats beside their plates. We sat at the counter by the window. Ben poured a stream of sugar from the shaker onto the marbled gray Formica and traced patterns in it. Icy chips of slush floated in the orange juice; my teeth ached as I sipped.

He walked me to the subway. "I'll call," he said, kissing me at the top of the stairs. I ran into the draft of the train rushing along the platform below.

Nina's note was taped to the fridge. *Gone home for the weekend. Your mother called.*

Sore and tired, I soaked in the benison of a hot bath, then crawled between my flowered sheets and napped until afternoon. When the silent phone and lonely apartment became unbearable, I bundled in my roommate's muskrat coat and walked to the Museum of Modern Art, to sit until closing among Monet's water lilies.

Back home, the telephone's sleek, silent surface mocked me. Just as I resolved to dial Ben, it rang. My mother's voice stretched thin across the wire. "I hope you didn't do anything foolish with that boy who called the other night."

"I slept on his sofa, safer than going home late."

"He should have brought you home. Don't throw yourself at him."

In the morning, I took the train uptown to 79th Street. I waited in the diner where we'd breakfasted, camouflaged behind the *Sunday Times* like a hunter in a bird blind, watching the blank windows on the fourth floor of his building.

Suddenly, he appeared — stepping into the diner, with a man.

"Hi, Ben," I said.

"Introduce us," said the man as though issuing a dare. He was large and handsome: black hair, black coat, gash of red scarf, like a Toulouse Lautrec.

"Sandy, this is April. An old friend from high school."

I had that feeling you have in dreams, the falling feeling.

"Serendipity, kismet," the man said, lips stretched into a narrow smile. "Two old friends bump into each other in the big city."

"Shut up," Ben said, dumping sugar onto the counter, tracing swirls in the fine grains.

"I'll leave you to your reunion. Surely you have a lot of catching up to do, after such a long time," the man said sarcastically.

Sandy pushed the door open with his shoulder and stood outside, staring at us through the window. Ben swept up a handful of sugar and tossed it at him. Sandy laughed as sugar spattered against the glass. Then he kissed the window, his lips spread like a sea anemone in an aquarium.

Ben exploded out the door, grabbing Sandy's scarf. Sandy unwrapped it, then twisted it around Ben's throat, pulling tight as if to choke him before letting go, kissing the scarf's fringe, tucking it in the neck of Ben's sweater, and walking away.

Head down as though leaning into a wind, Ben crossed Broadway. I caught up with him on the steps of his building.

"You owe me an explanation," I said, squeezing through the door, following him upstairs and into the apartment.

"Please, leave," he said, going into the bathroom and shutting the door.

The candles had burnt to nubs; the sink overflowed with dirty dishes. The red bed was rumpled. Ben's *pochades* still covered the sideboard. I chose the one of the Plaza fountain, slipped it in my coat pocket, and walked the twenty blocks home.

He never called, not even to accuse me of stealing. Or if he called, Nina didn't pass along the message. I phoned once, wanting at least to have it out. Sandy answered and I hung up.

Mesmerized, ambushed all these years later by the glittering tubes of paint, I imagined plucking *Chinese Vermilion* from the rack and slipping it in my pocket. My phone buzzed.

"Mom, what's taking you? I'm at the car. The food's getting cold."

"Be there in a minute." I turned away to find her display board.

Zoe unpacked our dinner with pride. "Look, Mom, Szechaun string beans." She doesn't eat anything green; she'd selected them for me.

Later, over a second beer, I picked up the newspaper and read an article about a neuroscientist studying grief. In brain scans a specific site lights up, activated by mourning; new loss starts all the old hurts throbbing, like a root canal gone bad.

When Charlie and I first married, I waved from the porch each morning as he left for work, as though we would be separated for a very long time — blessing him, protecting my beloved from disaster. But, finally, the disaster was in us, not out there. The commonplace enemy: time, familiarity, fatigue. When I found out about Sylvia, I wanted him to die, or to die myself; that seemed simpler, cleaner, than the mess of disentangling our lives. But Zoe demanded whatever flawed goods we could still deliver.

Turning to the alumni magazine, I studied the death notice again — obvious, between the lines, what the long illness that claimed him must have been. My good fortune, really, that it ended harsh and fast between us, good luck that my only souvenir was a stolen painting. Where was Ben's *pochade*? Lost, forgotten in some untidy drawer of my abandoned house. Now I wanted it back; I wanted everything back.

You could say Ben was practice, preparation. At least I got over him, the way you get over being young, if it doesn't kill you.

Shade Gardening

Nancy shut her son in his room every day after lunch. Three-year-old Jimmy did not like to nap, but she needed the break. Every day after lunch, after the same lunch of peanut butter and jelly and milk with pink strawberry syrup squirted in, she carried him to his room. Squirming, he was heavy to carry, but she was big and strong, a trans-planted farm girl. "If you lift a calf every day, pretty soon you can lift a cow," her father used to say.

"Don't squeeze me!" Jimmy cried each time she wrestled him to his bed.

She held his door shut while he hurled himself against it. Some-times they both cried, on opposite sides of the door; on bad days they both screamed until her throat was raw. When he subsided — often falling asleep on the floor by his door, other times whimpering and then humming as he drove his cars and trucks — she tiptoed away, crawled into bed, and lay there, leafing through her garden books, studying gar-dens she would never plant. A white garden to be seen by moonlight, a Shakespeare garden with every herb and flower annotated.

Today, though, she forced herself away from her soft bed. She would unpack the boxes that stood stacked against the living room wall, untouched since the move to Maryland. They'd moved in June, four months after the baby's death. Summer was over now, fall halfway gone. Benjamin would have been turning one at the end of this month, on Halloween.

"Do you want me to take a day off and unpack these boxes?" Rick had asked the night before. It was as close as he'd come to com-plaining. "Or do you need your mother to come out?"

"No," she'd said. "I'll take care of it. Tomorrow."

Jimmy had crayoned on the boxes. Scribbles and stick figures, yellow sun and green grass covered the brown cardboard, as though the boxes were the wall of a cave where the three of them were camping. Nancy approached the cartons warily; then, turning away, she pushed open the sliding glass door and went outside to weed the bluestone patio. Pesky little green shoots had sprouted up overnight, even though it was October.

A truck rattled up the gravel driveway and crunched to a stop. A young man jumped from the cab, lowered the gate on the rear, and lifted down a bushel basket: Nancy's special order of mixed daffodil bulbs from Holland.

"Leave them over there, please," she said, pointing to a sheltered corner by the house.

After the truck drove off, Nancy crouched by the basket, pried open the wire clasps, and removed the rough wooden top. The names on the packing slip were poetry — Cheerfulness, Golden Echo, Sun Disc, Lemon Drops. The bulbs, small, covered in husks of translucent skin, looked like shallots. She dug her hands in, sifting through the corms. How would she ever plant them all?

In June, Rick had offered to clear a corner of the shady property for a vegetable garden. She'd refused. "When we lived in the apartment you missed the farm, you wanted a garden," he'd said, exasperated. The dark shadows under his eyes made him finally look thirty. "Stop punishing yourself. What do you want?" he'd asked.

She didn't know.

She *had* wanted to leave Illinois, to escape the apartment on the top floor of the big old four-square in Champaign, just blocks from the university. The apartment — cozy when Rick started graduate school, when they were newlyweds — became cramped after Jimmy was born. Then sensitive, colicky Benjamin followed two years later. So tired she could barely lift her feet, she tripped over toys and shoes and books and dreamed of tossing the clutter out the window. For a hundred days after Benjamin was born, a hundred blurred days and nights, in a fog of fatigue and hormones, she had frightening visions of tearing the baby from her breast and throwing him out the window, too. Just after her internal clouds cleared, the baby died.

Mechanically, fueled by the adrenaline of fresh grief, Nancy boxed up all the baby stuff and gave it away. "Wait," her mother said,

"You might want it one day." Nancy did not want to see or touch any of it again.

Without the baby — with the changing table and the crib gone from the corner of their room, the mobile down, his drawers in her bureau emptied — the apartment seemed smaller and more crowded, not less. There was no place to be alone. She couldn't sleep, and if she finally dozed, night noises wakened her — wind whispering in the leaves, Rick's guttural snores. Jimmy's crying was the worst. She would jolt awake, sure for a moment it was Benjamin until remembrance settled like a stone, pinning her to the bed while Rick stumbled through the dark to comfort Jimmy.

Rick had interviewed at the laboratory at the National Institutes of Health in Bethesda before Benjamin died. His advisor had encouraged him: "You can always teach later, but now, with Kennedy, NIH is the land of milk and honey for basic research."

"Maybe it's not such a good time," Rick said when the offer came, three weeks after the baby's death, but Nancy told him to accept. "Wait," her mother said, disapproving and worried, though she'd come to stay with Jimmy while Nancy and Rick went east to house-hunt.

They'd taken the train to Washington, D.C., and rented a car. Rick drove her onto the NIH campus, proud as if he'd built it. The lab where he'd be working was on the tenth floor of a massive red brick building, at the end of a long corridor painted the pale, institutional green of hospitals. There was a hospital somewhere in this building, for studying diseases, finding cures.

"Welcome to Bethesda," said the lab chief, a plump, balding man. "We're so glad Rick's joining our team. Sylvie and I want you to come to our place tonight. We're barbecuing."

They'd planned to eat at a French restaurant in Georgetown, just the two of them.

"Thank you, but..." Rick began.

Nancy interrupted. "We'd love to." Rick smiled at her.

She excused herself to wait outside. Downstairs in the shadow of the building, she discovered a courtyard with a shallow rectangular pool and sat on the cool marble edge above the water. Lazy goldfish swam back and forth. Wasn't there a pool of Bethesda in the Bible? Nancy imagined dipping Benjamin's tightly furled toes in the water, immunizing him. He'd not lived long enough to run through a sprinkler on a hot summer's day.

The next morning a real estate agent showed them around. "What do you think, Nance?" Rick said after each house.

"It's fine. It would be okay." One had all pink appliances — stove, fridge, sink, even a pink toilet. "Your favorite color," Rick said, half teasing, half hopeful, trying so hard. The brick ramblers, the Cape Cods seemed interchangeable. The neighborhoods, too — hopscotch grids chalked on sidewalks littered with tricycles and strollers.

After they'd seen half a dozen houses, the agent said, "There is something else, not everyone's cup of tea. It's modular construction, the newest thing. Small, but you could easily add a room or two, when you have a second child."

Nancy did not explain that they already had two, depending on how you counted. *How many children do you have?* was a trick question.

The house was hidden from its neighbors in a grove of trees, pine and something else — tall primeval trees with square three-bladed leaves and big, showy yellow and orange flowers.

"What kind of tree is that?" asked Nancy.

"Those? Tulip trees. Tulip poplars," said the agent.

All glass and wood, the house looked like a child's drawing, a rectangular box with a sheltering triangular roof. Everything was on one level; no upstairs, no downstairs, no basement or attic. Outdoors and indoors were connected by a translucent membrane of floor-to-ceiling windows, flat sheets of glass. She'd never seen anything like this back home in the Midwest. The bare bones of a house, nothing soft or decorative. A blank slate. She was startled by a stab of longing.

"I like it," she said.

Rick grinned. "Sold," he said to the agent.

That evening they ate in the restaurant downtown. He told her not to worry about the price of the wine, or that the house cost more than they had planned. Later they made love. It was easier on the anony-

86

mous sheets of a hotel room without Jimmy next door and the shadows in the corner of their bedroom where the crib had been.

Nancy had whirled through the storm of packing up, eager to be done with good-byes, to be gone. As soon as the academic year ended, they left Illinois. But after the move, she missed the ready-made community of graduate students and wives, the potluck suppers migrating up and down the block, sitting on front steps drinking wine from paper cups, the mothers in her babysitting co-op who had taken Jimmy for days at a time after the baby died. She missed the casual conversations in the laundromat, or while pushing strollers to the corner playground. There were no sidewalks here, just looping roads and dead ends. She was marooned in the new development, built on what had once been farmland.

The lab chief and his wife hosted a crab feast to welcome them to Maryland. Jimmy had giddy fun slamming the wooden mallet down, leaving the work of picking out the meat to her. She'd never eaten crabs before and caught Rick watching as she sucked the briny, sweet meat out of the delicate legs. Afterward he and the other men shot baskets. Jimmy fell asleep in her lap as the wives sat on lawn chairs beside the improvised court on the asphalt driveway. At play, long legs and arms a blur of exuberant movement, her husband looked almost as young as their host's teenage son. Her reflection as she brushed her teeth before bed was flushed with beer and laughter. She'd forgotten Benjamin for a little while. The lapse felt like betrayal.

At the party, she'd heard about a co-op nursery school. Rick encouraged her. "It would give you a chance to meet people, some time to unpack, go downtown to the Smithsonian. You could drop me off and keep the car."

Nancy visited the school, in a church basement near NIH. The cheerful room was fragrant with apple juice, tempera paint, and paste. Jimmy sucked his thumb and buried his head on her shoulder during circle time. He clutched her skirt, frantic, when she started to leave. "He'll be fine," the kindly teacher said, and the helper mother nodded.

87

But she could not trust him to strangers, so the two of them continued to stay home alone.

Mornings she managed to be patient, blowing bubbles, mixing batches of play-dough, walking behind as he pedaled his trike round and round the circle of the cul-de-sac. But she could not sustain the effort past lunch.

Nancy knelt beside the basket of bulbs. It had been a miscalculation, getting so many — getting them at all. She put the lid back on the basket and wired it shut so squirrels would not eat them. Jimmy had been down for more than an hour. Her time was almost up. She pushed open the sliding door; it grated on grit from the sandbox, clogging the runner.

That evening she let the boy stand on a stool by the kitchen counter, wrapping scraps of bread dough around hot dogs. She nibbled a bit of raw dough. At first after the baby died, she'd lost weight until her clothes hung on her like hand-me-downs. Since moving she was eating, gaining weight, leaving waistbands unbuttoned and hiding her tummy beneath over-blouses, as if newly pregnant. And she desired sleep as if pregnant, dragging through the hours as though walking under water. But there was no chance of pregnancy. On the infrequent occasions she and Rick made love, she invariably used her diaphragm.

Rick's Volkswagen purred up the drive and pulled into the carport. He was early; he'd taken to staying late at the lab, losing himself in his work. She envied that.

"Daddy's home!" Jimmy toppled off the stool, running to greet his father, trailing flour across the speckled linoleum.

Nancy braced herself for her husband's disappointed glance when he discovered the sloppy barricade of boxes still untouched against the living room wall. She wanted him to say something, like he used to, and not be so careful.

But tonight was different. He wrenched open the sliding door and exploded inside, not saying hello, oblivious to the messy room, almost tripping over Jimmy. His expression was grim. Like that night at the hospital.

He shot toward the television, a little Zenith sitting in the corner on her grandmother's cedar chest, rarely used except for *Captain Kangaroo*. Reception was poor here. Bands of gray and black rolled across the screen.

"Damn," said Rick, banging the console. He never swore in front of Jimmy.

"Captain?" Jimmy asked doubtfully, squatting down and looking at the television, sucking his thumb.

Nancy recognized Kennedy's nasal voice. "The greatest danger of all is to do nothing. Aggressive conduct, if allowed to go unchecked and unchallenged, ultimately leads to war."

The hairs on her arms prickled. "What is it?"

"Khrushchev has missiles on Cuba. He could hit any city in the hemisphere. We're only twelve miles from the Capitol."

Nancy dropped down on the braided rug beside Jimmy. Rick banged the set again, and Kennedy appeared. Staring straight at her, he stated that Khrushchev's claim that the weapons were only defensive was a lie. Then the set sputtered; static filled the screen. Rick cursed again.

Nancy retreated to the laundry room beside the kitchen. Just a big closet, it was the only room in the house without windows. The dark cubbyhole was crammed with washer and dryer, suitcases, tools, beer, wine, canned goods, and Jimmy's tricycle. Nothing like the storm cellar her father kept ready for tornados, but this was all they'd have in the way of a fallout shelter.

She took two bottles of beer, put one in the freezer to chill for Rick and opened the other, drinking it warm as she pinched dough around the last hotdogs and slid the tray into the oven.

Rick was not giving up on the television. Kneeling, he fiddled with the antennae, wrapping them in aluminum foil. Jimmy pushed a car around the braided rug, using the circular pattern of the rag coils as his concentric highways.

"Bang!" he said as he crashed the car against his father's shoe.

"Don't bump me, buddy," Rick said, fierce with concentration, bending and angling the antennae.

After dinner, Rick bathed Jimmy. Nancy lay in their dark bedroom, listening to laughter and splashing water through the thin walls. Some nights, the cheerful sounds bothered her, though not tonight. The child, damp and shining, ran naked into the room. Rick captured and tickled him. Jimmy erupted in helpless giggles.

"Say goodnight to Mommy."

"Sleep here." His voice found the edge of a whine.

"How about we have story here, buddy?"

"Mike Mulligan," said Jimmy, curling up beside Nancy, his head on her pillow. She breathed the scent of baby shampoo as Rick read about Mike and his steam shovel Mary Anne, trapped safe and snug in their deep warm cellar.

"The end," Rick said. "Time for a piggy back to your big-boy bed."

Nancy went outside and sat on the lawn chair. Across the patio Jimmy's room glowed like a stage set. Since the baby died, Jimmy insisted on having the light on and keeping his father for company until his eyes closed. Sometimes Rick fell asleep first.

The light flicked off in Jimmy's room, then blazed in the living room.

"Nance?" Rick crossed the patio and sank into the other chair. "He asked who puts Benjamin to bed now," he said, his voice husky.

Jimmy rarely spoke of the baby. But since the move he'd refused to get his hair cut, and rejected new shoes. Once he had asked to go play with his best friend. "He's far away, honey. In Champaign," she said. "Like Benjamin," he said. She tried explaining the difference between far away and gone, reading him the book the pediatrician recommended, about the dead bird. He just sucked his thumb and closed his eyes.

"He still doesn't understand," she said.

"Neither do I," Rick said, bleakly, standing up. "I'm going next door, maybe they get decent reception."

"Don't leave."

"I'll be right back. We have to know what's going on."

His dark shape slipped through the trees between the properties. The flimsy open houses were beautiful lighted targets. A few miles away, the President and his brother must be talking about what to do. Were his children in bed?

Nancy went inside to check on Jimmy. He lay tangled in blankets, sweaty, clutching a truck in one fist. Maybe he would sleep through tonight.

That other night had begun like every night. After dinner, Rick gave Jimmy his bath and story and put him to bed. Then he walked back to his office on campus to grade papers; it was too chaotic to work in the apartment.

The baby had been even fussier than usual that day. He wouldn't nurse; he wouldn't sleep. Worn out, she paced the floor, holding him. He was hot, rigid, inconsolable. She felt afraid. Not of herself — the crazy, murderous thoughts were gone — but afraid for the baby. She stood by the window and looked out, hoping to see Rick. The pools of light beneath the streetlamps were empty.

Nancy called his office but there was no answer; he must be on his way home. She tried the rocking chair. The baby screamed on.

Jimmy padded from his room in footed pajamas, tousled and blinking. "Too noisy," he said, and stood by the chair, grasping her skirt with one fist.

Benjamin was burning up. She limped to the phone, holding the baby, towing Jimmy who would not let go of her skirt.

"Meet me at the hospital," said the doctor covering for her pediatrician. "Come in right away."

She left Jimmy with the downstairs neighbor and raced to the emergency room. The doctor thought it was an obstruction, or appendicitis. Benjamin died on the table before Rick arrived. The autopsy was inconclusive. They'd never be sure if there was something they should have known, something they could have done.

Now Nancy leaned over, inhaling the sweet moistness of Jimmy's sleep. Crossing the dark living room into her bedroom, she stretched out and dozed until Rick lay down beside her.

"Kennedy's sending the Air Force reserves to Florida. He's blockading Cuba."

"What's the point of that?"

"So they can't bring any more weapons onto the island."

"Locking the barn after the cows are gone?"

"Next door, they're packing to go to her family in Pittsburgh. Maybe we should go."

"Where?"

"Home."

"This is home," she said, surprising herself.

"To your folks."

"It's too far."

He didn't argue. They fell asleep holding each other.

Captain Kangaroo's cheerful voice woke her; she'd slept late. It was morning, the sun had come up and they were still here. A victory of sorts. Pulling on her robe, she went into the kitchen. Rick sat at the counter, reading *The Post.* She looked over his shoulder and read the caption beneath the grainy aerial photograph. *Sagua La Grande, Launch Pad with Erector.*

"Aren't you going to work?"

He shook his head. "Think I'll stay home. Help you with those boxes."

"My bulbs came. I need to plant them."

"Today?"

"Today," she said.

Dust motes danced in the warm air. Far above, the burnished canopy of tulip poplar leaves rustled. Soon the branches would be bare. What would a missile sound like, approaching? Would it be like the sinister whine of a wasp, or would it rip the sky open with a roar? She opened her gardening book to the planting instructions. Rick's shadow fell across the page.

92

"You're supposed to make the hole three inches deep, and fertilize with bone meal. But I forgot to get any," she said.

"I could go to the garden place."

The idea came like skywriting across a clear blue page. "We can use the ashes."

Rick wrinkled his forehead, doubt in his gray eyes. He'd let her have her way with the cremation, even though her mother, hurt that they had not brought the baby back to the family plot on the farm, said it was barbaric. Nancy had sprinkled a handful of ashes over the playground at the corner of campus before they moved away. The remainder, in the crematorium's box, wrapped with brown paper like an ordinary package, rested in her bureau drawer.

"I thought we were going to take him, the ashes, back to the farm, eventually," Rick said.

"I'll save some."

Nancy brought the box outside. Kneeling beside Rick, she opened it and rubbed a bit of the ashes between her fingers. "It's more like coral than ash."

They dug in silence, drizzling the fine, irregular crumbs of Benjamin's bones into the holes, dropping in the bulbs.

Jimmy came out on the patio. "I want to dig, too."

She went for a spoon. When she returned, her husband and son were kneeling over a box turtle. The edge of its shell was split and chipped, like a china saucer with a nick.

"Can I keep it?" Jimmy asked.

"Just for a little while," said Rick.

"Till it dies?"

They exchanged a glance over his head.

"Turtles live a long time. But they like to be outside," said Rick.

The turtle began to burrow into the leaves with scrabbling movements, as though swimming into the ground. Rick pulled Jimmy onto his lap.

"It wants to go to sleep underground," Rick said. "In the spring it will wake up, and we'll find it again."

Jimmy crawled away from Rick and poked his spoon into the box of ashes.

"No," said Nancy. "That's special sand. Just for grownups."

He looked up at her, squinting and mischievous, then dug his spoon in deep and flung it up, scattering a cloud of ash in the air. She shot out her hand to slap his spoon away, but pulled back, taking a breath.

"Just a smidge, Jimmy. Dig a hole for the bulb and then add just a little smidge."

The child soon lost interest, wandering off to drive his truck across the bluestone patio. She and Rick worked on, digging, sprinkling, burying the bulbs, surrendering to the rhythm of the task. After a while she put down her trowel and flexed her hands, cramped from digging in the red clay soil.

"They should flower next spring, right?" Rick asked. His strong freckled fingers patted the earth above a bulb.

She reached out and traced one of his knuckles with a finger. "Yes, next spring."

The sky overhead was a piercing blue, thrumming with the invisible energy of transatlantic phone calls, of offers and counter-offers. In the ground, the turtle and the bulbs were waiting.

The Bicycle Lesson

The door to the kitchen swung open. My mother carried in the birthday cake, her pale skin flushed in the candle glow, hair a frizzy gold halo around her plump face. Father followed, tall and angular, hunched over the bicycle he rolled into the dining room. It was lime green. A pink bow sat on the seat and a sign, *Happy Birthday, Lydia,* dangled from the handlebars. He snapped the kickstand down, parking the machine on the edge of the rug.

"Don't leave it there, dear," Mother said. The carpet, deep red and gold, had been in the truckload of furniture Grandmother Bradford, my father's mother, sent from her house on Beacon Hill when we moved to Maryland the year before.

I closed my eyes and blew out the candles, eleven. I opened my eyes. The bicycle was still there, right on the carpet where my father had left it; I had wasted my wish.

We ate my mother's marble cake topped with peppermint ice cream from Vinson's drugstore. The best ice cream in town was scooped behind their long marble counter; Mother must have walked there earlier, to have a quart hand packed. Peppermint was my favorite because tiny nuggets of candy lodged between my teeth, leaking clean sweetness after the ice cream was gone.

"Seconds, please," I said.

"Have mine," Father said, pushing his plate toward me. His cake was untouched, the ice cream melting. My mother shook her head, frowning. He had grown very thin again.

"You've barely eaten anything," she said to him, cutting a fresh piece of cake for me, topping it with the last of the ice cream. I ate slowly, to make it last. I knew what he would say when I finished.

"Let's take it out for a spin," he said as I put down my fork.

I had never ridden a bicycle; my grandmother said it was dangerous in Boston.

"What about training wheels?" I asked.

"You're too old for that nonsense. All it takes is practice."

97

I looked at my mother, but she glanced away, gathering the pink and white china plates. "Go ahead," she said, plucking cake crumbs from the lace tablecloth with her quick, delicate hands. She looked across the table at my father, fixing him in her steady gray gaze, a little wrinkle creasing her broad forehead. "Have fun."

"But of course," said my father, raising an eyebrow. Tonight the air around him crackled, like a hot night before a storm. He was excited. I wondered how long it would last, this time.

He wheeled the bicycle through the kitchen and onto what we called the back porch, though it faced the street. Years ago, another family had built the house for their vacation cottage, coming out from Washington for the cool summer breezes. The street was just an alley in those days and the driveway had been on the far side of the house, stretching down the hillside all the way to the Falls Road. Long before we came here the land behind us had been sold and houses built. We still had a big yard though, with a fishpond.

The house was a *bungalow,* Mother said. She kept a scrapbook of magazine pictures of houses, rooms and furniture. *My Dream Home,* she had written on the cover. Mother had never really had a home of her own, moving often as the child of a minister, coming East to go to college where she met my father, singing in the Harvard-Radcliffe Chorale. *We fell in love singing a Requiem. Maybe that should have told you something,* my father said. *If that's supposed to be a joke, it's not funny,* she replied. My parents graduated and married the same weekend, with her father performing the ceremony. Father went on to the Law School, and they moved in with his parents. It was meant to be temporary, just until he joined his father's firm. But my grandfather died and my father never joined his firm, or any other. Father had never worked even though his diplomas — Exeter, Harvard, Harvard Law School — marched up the stairwell in my grandmother's tall narrow townhouse, the house where I had always lived until we moved to Maryland so my father could go to the Lodge.

My new room was tucked under the eaves. A door opened out onto my own private screened balcony, *a sleeping porch,* Mother called it though I never slept out there; the insects were noisier than in Boston.

The room had a slanted ceiling; my father could not stand up straight in it. There were built-in shelves where I arranged my books in alphabetical order, leaving a space for my father's book, when he finished it. He had been writing a philosophy book since before I was born. My mother said if his parents had let him study philosophy instead of law, everything would have been different. He said, *Don't fool yourself. Don't torture me.*

Mother and I had still been in Boston for my April birthday the year before, and had celebrated without my father who was already in Maryland at the Lodge. The doctors there were the best in the world, my grandmother said, better than the ones he had tried at McLean, at Austen Riggs. Grandmother rented the house for us when his new doctor said it would be good to have his family close by. Mother agreed; she had worried even when he was only a few hours away in the Berkshires. But I found it easier, having him gone. I could make believe he was an ordinary father, on a long business trip, or even imagine that he was dead, and think how sorry everyone would be for me, half an orphan. I begged to stay in Boston with Grandmother — pretending I did not want to leave my school. Mother refused. *We shouldn't be separated,* she said. *He needs us, to get well.* It was always about what was best for him. School ended and we moved to Maryland.

The Lodge was only a few blocks from our house, on West Montgomery Avenue, a street of grand homes. *Victorians,* Mother called them. It seemed to me the families who lived in such big, solid houses behind gleaming bay windows must be happy.

Back in the days our house was built the Lodge had been a resort hotel. It still looked like one, from the street; the big brick building floated on a vast emerald lawn, shaded by tall chestnut trees. There was no fence around the property but two thick stone columns at the end of the broad drive marked the entrance. *Private,* said the engraved plaque on one. A trolley shelter stood by the entrance, the last stop on the line from Washington.

Father continued to stay at the Lodge for a time, even after we had moved, only coming home for occasional weekends, as he had in Boston. It was like having a houseguest when he visited. I felt as though

I was carrying a glass filled to the brim and had to be careful not to spill. The house had to be quiet, except for his piano playing. If I used my phonograph he would wince and say *Turn off that noise.* Some of my records played out of key, he said. He had perfect pitch; wrong notes bothered him that I could not even hear.

He lived with us full time after Christmas. That was how my mother put it, as though it were a job. She always had her eye on him. *He's doing well, Mother Bradford,* she reported to my grandmother, on the telephone. *He's sleeping all night.* Grandmother called every Sunday. *We shouldn't talk too long, I don't want to run up your bill,* my mother would say. My grandmother paid for everything.

Please don't tell me we will always be dependent on her for every breath we take, I heard Mother say to my father.

Do you have any idea how much I hate this? I've let you down, he replied.

It's not your fault, she said. *Work on the book. It will make you feel better.*

She had set up his desk in a corner of the dining room. He sat there sometimes, rolling sheets of blank white paper in and out of the typewriter, staring at the keys.

After he came to stay with us, Father walked to the Lodge each day. I could have kept him company, it was on my way to school, but I waited to leave until he was gone. Kids at school called the Lodge the nuthouse. There were cottages on the grounds where some patients lived; others stayed in halfway houses in the neighborhood, or rented rooms. I could always pick them out, shopping in town, or sitting at the soda counter at Vinson's. Some were obvious, faces twitching, with others it was something about their eyes. My father was different, in his three-piece suit and starched shirt. He could pass for a lawyer, except for the nights he did not sleep and sat up playing the piano and left for the Lodge the next morning in yesterday's wrinkled clothes.

The summer we moved to Maryland there was a Family Day at the Lodge, with tents on the lawn and a picnic dinner. My father introduced us to his doctor, a tiny little woman with gray hair. *So you're*

Lydia, she said with a strange accent. She was German; Father had told me she was Jewish and came to this country around the time I was born, because of the war. I wondered what he had told her about me. *You look like your father,* she said. People always said that, we were both tall and dark, and I was thin, like him, with his sharp nose, the Bradford nose. I wanted to ask her if she could make him better. And I wanted to ask, looking so much like him, what would happen to me?

He walked us around the grounds and showed us a cottage where he went to *Group* and talked to other people. He took us to the woodshop in an old barn where he was making my mother a jewelry box, decorating the top with a burnt design of leaves, dainty as lace. We saw the swimming pool, small, without a diving well. I could not imagine my tall father in the little pool, swimming around like a goldfish in a bowl. Still, it would have been convenient if my mother and I had been allowed to swim there on hot summer days. Instead we rode the trolley to Glen Echo Park to swim in the Crystal Pool. My mother said from the top of the high dive she could look over the trees and see the C&O Canal and down the Potomac River to Washington. I never climbed the diving tower but waited trembling below as her small figure streaked through the air and into the water; I held my breath until she surfaced, sleek and smooth as the seals at the Zoo.

Once my father came with us to Glen Echo. We had not been on an outing together since he was at the place in the Berkshires and had a weekend pass. *Time off for good behavior,* he had said. We had taken him to Tanglewood where all three of us lay on a blanket, listening to the symphony as the moon rose. *This is perfect,* he had said. *I wish I could freeze this moment and always be here with both of you.* Then he started to cry and my mother held him. The people on the blanket next to us said, *Quiet.* I left, pretending I needed to find a bathroom. When I picked my way back across the lawn, cannons were booming and my father was staring up at fireworks, his face pale in the glare, like the wild-eyed saints in paintings at the Museum of Fine Arts.

That day at Glen Echo, he tried to make me ride the roller coaster. *Leave her alone, you know she doesn't like heights,* my mother said. *You have to do what you are afraid of or it limits your life,* he said.

He rode the roller coaster alone, standing up despite the rules posted at the ticket booth. *Sit down,* Mother called. He just laughed and waved as he rocketed past; it looked as though the carriage might jump the frail wooden track. Later, at the Crystal Pool, he climbed to the top of the diving tower in his blue swimming trunks, ran out to the end of the swaying board, stretched onto his toes, and balanced for a moment before launching into the air. The diving board ricocheted with a loud twang. He shot down, sliced into the pool, and swam underwater all the way to the far end. Emerging, he shook himself like a retriever and ran back to the diving tower. Again and again he dove, springing higher off the board each time. People beside the pool clapped as though he were putting on a show; my mother watched him almost without blinking. At closing time the lifeguard had to pull him away from the ladder.

Father bought me a balloon as we left the park but the string slipped from my fingers and it floated away into the twilight like a pale second moon. *Lucky balloon,* he said, *making a break for it.*

Riding home on the trolley, half asleep between my parents, I wondered what my father was afraid of. I could not think of anything. Mother had told me that once when they were first courting he took her to Gloucester. She had learned to swim in the deep still quarries of Illinois and had never seen the ocean before. He swam out from the rocks into rough water as she watched from shore. *I was terrified, but he loved it,* she said. One day I had walked with him into town for an ice cream cone at Vinson's. We sat at one of the little marble topped tables and ate beneath the lazy draft of the ceiling fan. Finished, we left the sweet cool air of the ice cream parlor and followed the railroad tracks past the depot. An approaching train whistled. He winked at me and stepped onto the tracks. Kneeling down, he placed a penny on the rail, taking his time, then jumped back and stood beside me just as the hot breath of the train rushed past us. He retrieved the penny and handed it to me — a flat, thin copper wafer. *Don't tell your mother,* he said. We both knew her story of a little girl she had known in Illinois. The child, playing on the railroad track, was cut in two by one of the seventy trains that passed through every day. The girl's father, the town doctor, arrived at the accident and discovered it was his own daughter.

No, my father was not afraid of anything, so I knew he would not understand about the bicycle. But the night of my birthday, I hoped at least my mother would postpone the lesson.

"It will be dark soon," I said to her as he carried the bicycle down the porch steps.

"Not for awhile. Your father has been looking forward to this," she said. "Leave your pinafore with me." I turned around and she unbuttoned the stiff organdy pinafore I wore for special occasions. "Do you want a sweater?"

"No," I said. It was warm for April, but I shivered in my yellow checked dress, following him onto the driveway.

"Try her out for size," he said.

I clambered up onto the seat. My hands slipped on the grips.

"Pedal," he said.

Stretching my feet down, I pedaled in place as he held me.

"The seat's a little too high. Hop off," he said. I lurched over, pulling the bicycle after me.

He hurried down to the cellar, returning with his metal toolbox. Screwdrivers and pliers, hammers and wrenches, lay stored in neat rows, like sleeping soldiers, smallest to tallest. Choosing a wrench, he twirled the seat loose, adjusted it, and tightened the nut with his long-fingered hands. *Musician's hands,* my mother said. She tended his hands, massaging them with a special lotion of glycerin and rosewater, pushing the cuticles back with a stick of orangewood. I liked to sit beside him on the piano bench when he played, watching the arch of each finger. At bedtime I fell asleep upstairs, listening to him play, letting his music cover up the sounds of an old house at night — mice scurrying in the walls, radiators gurgling. Mother sang occasionally, and he accompanied her. Her songs were soft, like lullabies. *These Lieder are too sweet for my blood. It makes you want to smother a baby,* he said once and I pulled my pillow over my ears. Many times I awakened in the middle of the night and heard crashing chords, loud as thunder. Perhaps my grandmother should not have given us the grand piano. It was too big, almost filling our parlor.

Father replaced the wrench in the toolbox. "Now this steed

should fit like it was custom grown." He pinched the tires. "Always make sure you have the right air pressure," he said, unscrewing the little black plastic cap on the front tire. "You don't ever want to lose these," he said, tucking the cap in his breast pocket. He unhooked a shining cylinder from the bicycle frame, extracting its tiny hose and fitting it over the tire valve. He pumped, squeezed the tire again, and screwed the valve back on.

"That's more like it. Let's take her over to the Academy."

I lagged behind as he rolled the bicycle down the drive. The Academy was on the corner where our street met West Montgomery Avenue. A tall brick building with a tin roof, it had been a school at the time of the Civil War and now it was the Library. Its small parking lot was empty at this hour.

"What are you waiting for? An engraved invitation?" he said, patting the seat.

I hoisted myself onto the precarious perch.

"Pedal," he said. "I've got you." I pushed down once and stopped. "Come on," he said. "I won't let you fall."

We took off, my father jogging behind me, pushing me across the parking lot. The front wheel shimmied.

"Stop!" I screamed. He ran faster, as though he had not heard. I yanked my feet from the pedals and threw myself off the bicycle, tangling my legs in the frame as it crashed down. He pulled the bicycle upright, leaving me on the ground.

"Next time you want to stop, try braking," he said, frowning. He hopped on the bicycle. It was much too small for him, he looked like a circus clown, pedaling in circles around me, ringing the shrill chrome bell, whistling and grinning. What if someone I knew came by? "Just press back on the pedals like this and you stop," he said, jumping off, bowing and brandishing an imaginary top hat. "Your turn, mademoiselle." He looked down at me, eyes glittering, his face a strange grinning mask. "All it takes is practice. Once you have it, you are going to love it. It's like flying."

I huddled on the ground beside the bicycle. My knee was bleeding, my dress torn and smudged with grease.

"Get back on, or it will be harder next time," he said in a harsh voice. I closed my eyes and hunkered down like a turtle in its shell. Licking the salty blood from my throbbing knee, I did not look up until I heard the bicycle roll away. I followed at a distance down the dusky street.

Mother was on the porch swing, knitting. I sat beside her while he put the bicycle away. "How did it go?" she asked. I sniffed the liquid in her china cup — sherry from the bottle hidden in the back of the pantry. "Rome wasn't built in a day," she said, draining her drink as he came up the steps. "That's a nasty scrape, let's go clean it up."

She filled the deep claw-foot tub and poured in bubble bath, unbuttoning my dress without speaking. I sank into the fragrant cloud of foam and lay still. My knee stung. She sat on the edge of the tub.

"If I could do it, it would make him happy," I whispered.

She stroked my hair, kissed the top of my head, and left the room, carrying the spoiled dress. It could be laundered and mended, but there would always be a jagged scar where it had ripped. I would shove it to the back of the closet, not wear it again.

Mother was speaking to him, in the hallway outside the bathroom door. "Be patient. You of all people should understand." I scrunched down in the tub and let water fill my ears. Squinting at the surface of the water, I watched the tiny bubbles pop, one by one.

After my bath, I sat on the sleeping porch. Below, the dogwood tree shimmered silver in the moonlight. There was a faint sweet scent of lilacs in the air. A train whistled, sad and low as a sigh. I was still damp, chilly in my thin cotton gown, so I went back inside, crawled into bed and dozed. Later, the sound of the piano woke me. My mother flitted past my door and down the stairs, like a shadow in her gray bathrobe. "Please, darling, come to bed," she said. The music pounded, louder. He was still playing when I fell asleep.

The next morning the smell of burnt toast woke me. I came down to breakfast; my father sat at the table in his clothes from the day before, staring at the front page of *The Post*. I pierced the yolk of a poached egg and watched the thick yellow bleed out onto the toast.

"I don't feel well," I told my mother.

105

She laid her cool hand across my forehead. "You'll be fine once you get to school."

He did not look up or say goodbye when I left and was gone when I came home that afternoon. "The doctor thought it would be good for your father to have a little rest at the Lodge," she said.

Mother had me set the supper table in the kitchen, not the dining room, since it was just two of us. She made macaroni and cheese, with toasted breadcrumbs on top, my favorite. I pushed the noodles around my plate. What were they serving for supper at the Lodge? Was he hungry or was this one of those times he would not eat or sleep?

My mother stood behind me, touching my shoulder. "There's leftover birthday cake," she said. I shook my head.

After dinner, I put on my oldest corduroy trousers — the knees already patched, the seat worn smooth — and went to the garage. My bicycle gleamed in the dim light. I kicked the front tire, grabbed the handlebars and wheeled the machine outside. Leaving the bicycle propped against the house, I straddled the seat. Pressing down on one pedal, I pushed off with the other foot and propelled myself along, scooter-style, scraping against the side of the house. The handlebar left a gray streak along the stucco. Arriving at the corner of the house I dismounted and turned the bicycle around. I repeated the experiment, over and over.

The next evening I practiced again, using my new method, letting the house hold me up. This time upon reaching the corner I did not stop. Drawing my pushing foot up onto the pedal, I let the bicycle roll free of the supporting wall, down the sloping driveway. My hands shook; the bicycle teetered and lurched into the boxwood hedge. Branches scratched my face and arms, breaking my fall. I rested a moment, inhaling the spice of crushed boxwood, then staggered upright, pulling the bicycle out of the hedge. I plucked twigs from the spokes and pushed the bicycle back up the driveway. Throwing myself on before I could change my mind, I catapulted down the drive, almost reaching the street before crashing onto the pavement, grinding my palm into gravel. I hauled the bicycle upright, rolled it back up the driveway, and launched down the slope again, making it all the way onto the street. I pedaled and picked up speed until I was flying, just as he had promised. At the Academy parking lot I capsized, but I climbed back on, rode home and jerked to a stop on the soft lawn. Mother ran down the porch steps and hugged me. My heart pounded, my blood fizzed like ginger ale.

Every evening that week I practiced, and all Saturday afternoon, until I was in control of the machine, perfect and steady. Sunday morning I pedaled down our street and turned onto West Montgomery. The big yellow and white houses passed in a blur as I sped by, ringing my bell. At the Lodge I turned in, following the smooth drive as it unrolled beneath the canopy of chestnut trees. I approached the main building. Four stories tall, a turret at one corner, it looked almost like a castle, except for the bars on all the narrow windows above the second story and the fire escape zigzagging along the wall. Flipping down the kickstand, I parked, climbed the broad staircase, and tugged on the front door. It had stood wide open the day of the family picnic but was locked now. I heard piano music and ran along the porch to find my father. Peering in a long French window I saw a fat woman with white hair, playing with her eyes closed. I turned away and almost bumped into a man who had crept up behind me. "Pretty," he whispered, reaching out toward me. I batted his hand aside and darted past him down the steps to my bicycle.

Then across the lawn I saw my father's thin figure. He was walking stooped over, like an old man. He inched along the path toward the woodshop, followed by a woman in white. I rode toward him, ringing the bell, *Ching, ching, ching.* It sounded loud as a fire alarm in the hush of the green park but he did not look up. I swerved and almost crashed, braking to stop just in front of him. He stared at me with dull eyes.

"You were right," I said. "It's wonderful."

"So you managed without me." He leaned over and kissed me; his breath smelled sour. I stepped back. He shrugged and walked away along the path toward the woodshop.

"Wait," I called. "When are you coming home?" Father paused and looked back; he lifted one hand but then dropped his arm as though it were too heavy to wave. He disappeared into the barn.

"No visitors," said the nurse. "Run along."

My legs ached on the ride home.

The next day my mother suggested I bicycle to school, but I walked. The sherry bottle was in plain view on the kitchen table when I arrived home that afternoon; my mother was leaning on the sink, her back to me. She turned, her eyes scorched holes in a paper-white face. Taking a deep breath, she began to speak. "There was an accident at the Lodge," she said in a flat voice. She inhaled again, as though preparing to dive. "Your father fell from a fire escape," she said, opening her arms. I stumbled across the kitchen and burrowed into her. She shivered although wearing a heavy sweater she had made for my father; the rough wool scratched my face. Holding onto her as though we were drowning, I began to sob.

"Go ahead and cry," she said. "I wish I could."

So I wept, it was all I could do for her. Mother cradled me in her arms, rocking back and forth. I gulped in her mingled fragrances of rosewater, sherry, and lanolin from the wool sweater. The phone rang; she stepped into the hall to answer, pulling the kitchen door shut after her. Hovering behind the door, I listened to the indistinct murmur of her voice, stepping away as she returned.

"Your grandmother is taking the train from South Station tonight, she will be here by morning."

The doorbell chimed; I hung back in the kitchen as she greeted the minister from the Presbyterian Church on West Montgomery. We had gone there just a handful of times. How had he known already? I slipped out the back door. The sunlight was too bright; I crept into the dark cave of the garage where the air was heavy with the sweet smell of oil and gasoline. Kneeling beside my bicycle I unscrewed the valve caps from the tires, tossing them away. I waited for the tires to collapse with a gush of air. Nothing happened; my father's caution and warnings had been pointless. I mounted the bicycle and rode fast toward the Lodge, as though I would be in time to see him, as he stood on the fire escape, stretching up on his toes, preparing to dive, preparing to fly. As though, if I hurried, I could catch him as he fell.

White Laurel

Priscilla shifted the glossy laurel leaves in the big vase on the lobby table to reveal the white blossoms. Everything must be perfect tonight.

The cook and the waitress stopped talking when she walked into the kitchen. The air was warm and heavy with cooking steam. Her glasses fogged, she slipped them off to dangle on the chain around her neck.

"Good evening, Joyce. Everything alright?" she said.

"Yes, ma'am."

She opened a cutlery drawer and selected a spoon. Standing at the huge range she stirred Joyce's gravy, checking for lumps.

She asked, "Relish trays ready, Annie?"

"Almost, Mrs. Crichton."

She would have preferred a more experienced, older waitress, particularly tonight. Annie was too young, her uniform too snug. Finding good help had never been easy here in the country and had grown harder over the years. She knew she had a reputation for being difficult but she had maintained her standards. After tonight, she need not worry about waitresses again.

She pushed through the swinging door into the dining room. The dove gray walls, white table linen, the soft glow of pewter and warm heart-of-pine floors pleased her, as always. The stage was set. This was her favorite moment — everything ready, undisturbed by guests and food.

Sixty years ago, the first time she sat at a table in this room, her feet had not touched the floor. She remembered swinging her legs until the Windsor chair jiggled; she remembered her mother's impatience.

"Priscilla, sit still."

"Let me take her out for a little walk while we wait."

She held her father's hand and he let her swing their joined arms high and hard. He took her outside to the bowling alley in the long

111

narrow wooden shed. He stood beside her, placed her hand on the ball, and guided her arm back and forward,

"Now, let it go!"

The ball rolled down the wooden floor, the shed echoed with soft musical thunder and the wooden pins fell in glorious, noisy cascade. He promised her a real game after dinner, and kept his promise. He kept every promise. Each summer until she was eighteen she and her parents took the train from Pittsburgh for a week's sojourn at the inn. Few children stayed there. Priscilla and her father bowled, played croquet and tennis, and rode horseback along the trail to the quarry to swim. Her mother read undisturbed on the wide porch.

Now, a lifetime later, she stepped onto that same porch. The western sky was beginning to glow through the hemlock branches. She waited as she had almost every evening for forty years — waited for guests to come to her little valley, William's Cove as locals called it, after the first tavern keeper, two hundred years ago.

The grandfather clock in the hallway chimed once, marking the half hour, five thirty. The moon on the clock's painted face would chase the sun down across the dial as outside the evening fell and the moon rose. She returned to the dining room for a final inspection, circled the tables, straightening a fold of linen, lifting a goblet and polishing off a speck of dust. She had taken even more than her usual care with the flowers tonight. Sprays of crimson sheep laurel with narrow, graceful leaves floated in crystal bowls on the tables, white mountain laurel stood sentry in the big vase on the cherry sideboard. It had been beautiful in the woods today, walking slowly up the mountain, harvesting her blossoms for the last time.

She placed a *Reserved* sign on the table by the west window, selected for the view across the road toward the pavilion over the spring. The reservation sign was not necessary, but there would be a few other diners tonight, sentimental or just curious. She wished the room would be full just this once more, filled with murmurs, muted laughter, and the music of silver on china. She would orbit her orderly universe, making sure all was well, saying farewell.

She hoped the buyer would not close the Inn for long. Dust

would silt the polished floors, vines would encroach upon the paths, hemlock needles would sift down and clog the gutters. Just a brief break for inventory, and some minor renovations, the realtor said.

The room looked well tonight and she knew she did, too. First time visitors were often surprised to find such atmosphere, such a hostess, three hours from Pittsburgh. She had gone into town this afternoon and had her hair done. She no longer went weekly. In the beauty shop's bright lights she looked every bit of her seventy years; she did not like to confront her gray hair in the beautician's large mirror. At least she had not gone gray early, like her father. He had joked that his iron gray hair matched the source of the family fortune. The fortune was gone now; some poured into this Inn, more wasted by her husband Parker's poor stewardship.

Parker. She remembered the dinner party in honor of her graduation from Bryn Mawr.

"Let me introduce my new right hand man, Parker Crichton. Parker, my daughter Priscilla."

"Lovely to meet you, Priscilla. I have admired your paintings in the office. You are most talented." He shook her hand, and held it a moment. Her heartbeat roared in her ears as though magnified by a seashell. The chatter of the party around her faded in the surf until her father's voice pulled her to shore.

"Parker is from Philadelphia. Priscilla won an award in a competition at the Art Institute."

"A *student* competition, Father."

"Perhaps you could show me the Carnegie Institute one day, Priscilla."

And so began the summer of their courtship. He, ten years her senior, was so at ease with the ritual of wooing. It was like dancing in the arms of an experienced partner, a relief after the awkward, uncertain attempts with earnest young men from the University or Haverford. She remembered that summer as a time of delights — tea dances, concerts, picnics in Schenley Park, rides up and down the Incline. Beneath the froth of activity was desire. They often strolled through the Carnegie, dim and quiet in that time. One day, in a gallery overcrowded with

113

Greek statuary, they paused before a marble tableau, Apollo pursuing Daphne. The sculptor had caught the moment of her escape, her magical metamorphosis into a white laurel tree. Long toes sprouted root tendrils, breasts tipped up and budded, slender arms stretched, fingers turning into twigs.

"After he lost her, Apollo made the laurel sacred," she said.

"Sweet classics major, did he bring other nymphs to picnic beneath her branches?" He reached out a hand and ran it down Daphne's marble thigh.

"The guard will see you."

"He'll understand, I couldn't resist," he said, reaching out for Priscilla's hand.

The first summer they owned the Inn he persuaded her to rename it.

"Magnesium Springs Inn is too medicinal. We'll attract more tourists with something pretty, besides you." So it became the White Laurel Inn, after the white blossoms sprinkling the mountainside like confetti.

She left the dining room, passed through the hall, crossed the wide threshold to the porch. Wide gray floor boards stretched out on either side, the ceiling was blue to repel wasps according to local custom. Twenty empty rocking chairs sat poised at the rocking rail. Only the gentlest toe tap, the slightest exertion was required to initiate perpetual gentle motion on languid summer afternoons. She sat and rocked, stretching and flexing her aching fingers. Her hands were ravaged by arthritis, roped with veins, but the engagement ring, the mysterious fire opal, still glinted. He had paid for it from the wages he was earning from her father. She remembered laughing toasts at their wedding, sly innuendo about marrying the boss's daughter. By the time she had been ready to stop wearing the ring, she could not pull it over the swollen knuckle.

Gravel crunched in the circular drive. A sleek gray car pulled to a stop, elegant, expensive. Parker would have known the make, model and cost, at any distance.

A man stepped out, tall, broad shouldered, about forty. He

114

wore khaki pants, a soft green jacket — cashmere, possibly, a good choice, for the cool June evenings. Parker had judged guests by cars, she by clothes. She stood up, prepared her smile, and descended the porch steps. The discipline of decades of professional hospitality would see her through tonight.

"Welcome to the White Laurel Inn."

"I've been looking forward to this evening."

He held out a bouquet of hothouse roses, long stemmed, deep red. Out of season and out of place, she thought.

"Thank you, how beautiful."

"And this." He presented a cool, wet-skinned bottle of champagne, Moët. When had she last felt dry bubbles dance along her tongue and down her throat? It was a young person's drink, not like the comfort of sherry in the evenings. Champagne was for beginnings, weddings, christenings, launchings. Perhaps she should smash the bottle against the porch railing.

"What a lovely gesture."

"Well, this is quite an occasion."

"Yes, it is."

"I've been looking forward to meeting you, seeing the place again. It was raining the day the agent showed me around. But I fell in love, on first sight."

"Would you like to take a walk, before dinner? Let me have one of the girls in the kitchen prepare us a hamper for cocktails. We'll take your champagne."

She stepped inside, and realized she had neglected to ask him in. This time tomorrow it would be his prerogative to invite her. Let him wait on the porch tonight. In the dining room she selected a cut crystal vase for the roses, then pushed through the swinging door into the kitchen.

"Oh, ma'am, what beautiful flowers," said Annie. She would let the little waitress take the bouquet home, once he was gone this evening.

"Put them in this vase, and then on the piano in the lounge. Be sure the bottom of the vase is quite dry. And put this bottle in a picnic basket, with two glasses, wrapped carefully, please, in napkins. And some of the melba toast and cheese straws Joyce made today."

"Yes, ma'am."

The girl was breaking in, with more time she might have become satisfactory. The uniform really was too snug, remarkable breasts on such a slender girl. She remembered the first time she caught Parker's eyes following the waitress Carol across the dining room. She had held a heavy round tray of dishes aloft with strong, smooth arms, uniform strained across generous bosom and hips. She pivoted on muscular legs, pushing the swinging door open with her full bottom. He stared at the door a moment after she disappeared into the kitchen and then smiled, "A buxom wench, my dear. These farm girls." She had smiled back. His admiration was just reflex, like stroking the marble Daphne's flank.

"I'll be back in a minute, Annie. Wrap the glasses carefully."

She went upstairs for a sweater. Her suite of rooms was stripped for tomorrow, private possessions in boxes, ready to ship to Pittsburgh. Everything else in the rest of the Inn was to convey. It was simplest that way, and after all, the Inn was the intended setting for her careful collection of local antiques. Her paintings would remain, too. She had portrayed the white clapboard inn, the weathered outbuildings, the mountainside and streams in every season, in watercolor and in oil. Her paintings were portraits of this place; the place itself had been her real masterpiece, never quite captured on canvas.

Her bare room looked stark and simple, a Shaker cell with pine bed and empty bookcase. The wide floorboards squeaked as she crossed into the bathroom. She looked tired in the unforgiving glare of the light above the mirror. She stroked soft red across her thin lips, then opened the jewelry box and took out her pearls. She fastened them, remembering Parker's hands closing the clasp, stroking a finger down her neck. "I look forward to taking these off, later," he whispered.

She stood before the glass. She had read in *National Geographic* that pearls gain luster with wearing, and that somewhere poor women with particularly desirable skin oils are hired to wear pearls, to give them a fine patina. How could those women give up the pearls they had fostered? These had been hers for forty-eight years this month. She and Parker had come to celebrate their first anniversary here, where they had honeymooned. Early evening light filtered through hemlock branches outside the window. She was sitting at the dressing table, brushing her hair, wondering what to wear to dinner.

"Happy anniversary, darling," he had said, and reached a long narrow box from the pocket of his dressing gown. He opened it and drew out a string of luminous little moons. He slipped them on, fastened the clasp, and bent and kissed her nape. She turned to him, silk kimono falling open. He lifted her from the dressing table bench and carried her to bed. They made love on heavy linen sheets, in the warm light of evening, hidden by the fringed curtain of hemlock from the bright-eyed squirrels.

She grimaced, checking her teeth in the mirror to make sure there was no smear of lipstick. She walked down the broad staircase, running her hand along the satin of the banister.

"Do you have the hamper ready, Annie?"

"Yes, everything, just like you said."

She turned to the cook.

"Joyce, I am taking Mr. Redmond on a tour of the grounds. We will be back by seven, before any guests arrive. If anyone comes before I return, please have Annie seat them in the Lounge with some Melba toast, a relish tray."

"Yes, ma'am."

She stepped out the back door into the sunroom. She had created it years ago from the little back porch, installing tall casement windows and a Franklin stove. The windows were left open all summer, but closed in the fall. Then she brought her bright terra cotta pots of begonias inside, lit the stove and the room glowed like a lantern, attracting late moths to the windows. She could crack open the windows and send Parker there for his cigar, if it was too cold for his after dinner walk. She had liked the heavy sweet aroma of cigar smoke and could trace him by scent like a bat following echoes.

She walked through the herb garden, planted in one of the few sunny spots on her shady property, and around to the front. The man was rocking on the porch, head resting against the chair's high back.

"These chairs are marvelously comfortable."

"Local oak and hickory, bent and steamed. They still make them, but ours are more graceful than the newer ones. Longer backs, longer rockers."

"May I carry the basket for you?"

"Thank you. This way."

They stepped off the porch onto the circular drive and crossed the road. She led him down moss-covered steps, across the log bridge, over the first stream.

She stood by the entry to the pavilion over the spring. It was always dark and damp inside.

"Step onto the boardwalk inside, the floor is wet."

He followed her in.

"The water comes up out of the ground over there."

He read aloud from the sign she had painted in black on a white board.

"You are on Hallowed Ground. Indians met here to make Peace. You are Welcome to Spring Water but don't waste cups."

She pulled a paper cone from the cup dispenser nailed beside the sign. Careful not to get her hem wet, she bent and filled the cup. She handed it to him.

"To your health, and to the health of the Inn."

"Whew, some bouquet."

"Minerals. Magnesium, sulphur. I first drank it as a child and as you can see, I've lived a long life."

He spilled the water back onto the wet stones without sipping.

"Shall we go on?" she asked.

"Lead the way."

They walked along the fragrant pine needle path to a long brown shingled shed, the bowling alley. She climbed the steep stairs and unlocked the door.

"We keep it locked now. Local kids."

She did not tell him they still broke in, she still awoke at night

118

to the raucous thunder of laughter and bowling balls. She would not miss coming into the bowling alley on mornings after it had been violated, finding the wooden trough that carried the balls back down between the two long lanes broken, the pins sprawled, spent condoms in the corner by the heavy old mission sofa, and puddles of beer leaking onto the scarred hardwood floor. The worry would convey, that would be his now.

"Dark in here," he said.

She flipped the switch but it was still dim at the far end of the lanes. The floor creaked as he walked across to read the sign,

"Bowlers must set their own Pins unless
Pin Boys are arranged for in Advance."

"What are those little booths at the end of the lanes?"

"The pin boys sat there, to protect their legs."

She walked to the end of the lane and arranged the pins in neat formation. Then she climbed into the pin boy pulpit and sat, looking down the dusty alley. As a child she liked to set the pins and perch here to watch her father's ball roll down the lane and smash the pins into a roaring avalanche. She would jump down from the roost, reset the soldierly pins in stiff formation, and roll the heavy ball back to her father on the raised wooden viaduct between the lanes.

"You came here, as a child?"

"Every summer, with my parents. And on my honeymoon."

"How did you decide to buy the place?"

"I didn't. My husband decided, and gave it to me."

"Some surprise."

"Yes. He liked to surprise me."

Parker had been master of the grand gesture. They had come to spend Christmas at the Inn, after a hard autumn. Her father had died; she had miscarried. They took long sleigh rides through the woods and read beside the fire in the lounge. She slept more easily than in weeks at home. Christmas morning she awoke to the gray dawn of another snowy day.

"Santa Claus left this for you," he said, handing her a large manila envelope. She drew out a document. It was the deed to the Inn.

"Merry Christmas, darling. Now you have scenery to paint and rooms to decorate."

A bowling ball thundered down the lane, right for the heart of the phalanx of pins.

It hit and the pins exploded, pulling her back to the present moment.

"Strike!" He straightened, pleased with his marksmanship. "Hey, that's fun. Brighter lights, an electric pin setter, and we're in business."

"Let's go on."

They continued on the broad pine needle path above the stream.

"Over there is the croquet lawn. Beyond it, the clay tennis court." She realized the lawn had not been cut and looked ragged. The tennis court had not been rolled, weeds sprouted, and the net sagged. She didn't take this path often.

"You kept people busy, relaxing."

"I suppose."

They came to the garage. He walked up and peered in.

"That's a gorgeous old Packard in there."

"Yes, it was one of my husband's cars. It has not been driven in a long time."

They walked on to the barn.

"Six stalls."

"Do you keep horses?"

"No, not any longer. We did. These trails are beautiful on horseback, up the mountain, into the cove. Let's walk out to the lake."

The first summer they owned the Inn, Parker had engineered the lake in the glen where three mountain streams converged. He gloried in the project when he came out from Pittsburgh, weekends. She was living at the Inn fulltime, just until she could find a reliable manager, they agreed. They liked to plunge into the water on hot afternoons and swim out to bask on the floating dock and watch glistening dragon flies swoop and fly, coupled, low across the water. She could not find a manager, and stayed on in the fall. They kept canoes by the lake

120

and paddled in water ablaze with the reflection of foliage and blue sky. Winter came, and she remained, and by Christmas week, the lake froze. Weekends, Parker built fires in the open fieldstone hearth in the bathing pavilion and began the annual custom of skating parties. Guests and even some locals came to skate and sit by the fire and drink hot cider at the round table she had made from an old millstone.

She led him to the bathing pavilion. She noticed fresh ashes and trash in the fireplace. The kids would burn the place down one day.

"Here we are. Let's have our cocktails here."

He set the basket on the millstone table. She unwrapped the glasses and handed him the cool, green bottle.

"Would you open this?"

He pointed the neck out toward the water and laughed as the cork shot out.

"Here's to the Inn!"

He poured frothy liquid into the glasses, and handed her one. She took a sip. The sharp, spicy bubbles tingled on her tongue and down her throat. Her eyes smarted. She walked to the water's edge. The surface was grown shut, green with algae and lily pads. It looked almost solid, as though you might step out on it. She had neglected this spot for a long time.

She had never been able to find someone she trusted to manage the Inn, and so she stayed on, and he spent workweeks in Pittsburgh. As the years passed Parker had to travel more on business trips, to Chicago, Detroit, Cleveland, and could not come to the Inn each weekend. When he traveled as far as San Francisco he was gone for a month, and asked her to come with him, but she could not, absorbed by the cares of the Inn.

"I'm jealous; you love this place more than me," he teased.

"No, but you can take care of yourself. I'm needed here."

Each day began with an early morning ride along the serpentine path through the deep hemlock grove on the mountainside. She returned in time to oversee the guests' breakfast of fresh eggs, thick slabs of bacon, pancakes with syrup from native maples. Breakfast required her supervision, she explained to Parker, recounting the morning she overslept and the cook beat the blueberries in the batter until they split, staining batter and muffins blue. After breakfast she would paint, usually in the studio Parker had made for her in a shed behind the bowling alley. He had replaced the entire north wall with windows to capture as much light as possible in the deep hemlock shade. Occasionally after breakfast she would have the cook pack her a box lunch and leave the waitress in charge of the dining room for luncheon. Then she would take her canvas stool, folding easel, and paints and ride to the old quarry deep in the cove between the mountains on the farthest border of her property. Before Parker made the lake, the quarry had been the only place for swimming. As a child, she had learned to swim in its clear dangerous depths, her father treading water close beside her. No one visited here now. She set up her easel and painted until the sun was high. Then she stripped and swam naked in the cool, deep water. Tingling, she crawled out and ate lunch. She baked herself on the warm rock shelf beside the quarry, drowsed in the sun, thinking of Parker.

That long ago June, Parker had been away almost a month. She woke in the middle of the night to gravel crunching beneath her window as a car purred to a stop. She waited, expectant. He slipped into bed beside her, hair redolent of cigar smoke and pomade, and rolled her into his arms. He ran his fingers up under her nightgown, between her thighs. "Did you miss me?" he whispered, "Do you want me?" She came, even before he entered her and completed the sweet heavy embrace of reunion.

The next day was busy; they had almost a full house. She did not need to see Parker to feel his presence all day. She heard his confident step on the porch, his jovial voice in the lounge as he charmed the guests with stories. The Inn gleamed, freshly painted that spring. Outside white clapboard sparkled against the green hemlock. Inside, the dining room was dove gray, a soft backdrop for the dull glow of her pewter collection. She had arranged a big urn of dark, glossy rhododendron leaves in the lobby. The burnished leaves shone against the forest green walls. Her favorite of her paintings, the spring pavilion, hung above the reception desk, beside the wall of pigeonholes for mail and keys. Parker teased that soon she must stop painting or he must buy a bigger place with more walls.

The day went well. They had two seatings for dinner. Parker escorted the last diners down to the basement recreation room. She pretended to disapprove of his informality, his familiarity with the guests, but knew his warmth was the perfect foil for her rectitude. They were a good team. She listened to ping pong balls and laughter ricochet off the stone walls downstairs as she put the silver away in the dining room. She kept charge of that task; country girls were incapable of learning the difference between fish forks and salad forks. Soon it would be quiet, the help gone home, the guests to bed. She craved quiet at the end of days full of people, demands, obligations.

Parker came in and said, "They are enjoying themselves down there."

"So I heard."

"Think I'll go smoke and stroll. Care to join me?"

"No, I'll finish this, then practice awhile."

She liked to play the piano after dinner, if there were no guests in the lounge playing cards. She needed a little solitude, and some time to practice. Both were hard to come by, when he was home.

He kissed her and pushed through the swinging door into the kitchen. She knew he would pass on to the sunroom, find a cigar in the humidor she kept for him there, and then take his walk. She finished putting away the silver and surveyed the dining room. Carol had prepared it well for breakfast, the heavy sprigged coffee cups were inverted on saucers, fresh cloth napkins were fanned in water goblets. Yes, she had finally trained a good waitress. She might be able to accompany Parker to San Francisco the next time and leave the Inn in Carol's care. She turned off the lights and stepped into the kitchen. The new cook was improving also. She now seemed to almost understand cream sauces and lightly cooked vegetables.

"Good night, ladies. Thank you, see you in the morning."

She crossed the lobby to the lounge, found it empty, and opened the piano. The piano had been his gift to her on their tenth anniversary.

"You say everything here must be beautiful and useful. Well, something beautiful. Put it to good use."

Even for him, arranging the secret delivery of a Steinway grand from Pittsburgh along the narrow mountain road into their cove must have been difficult. The piano had grown ever more beautiful to her with years of use. She stroked the smooth ivory keys and opened her book, Chopin nocturnes. The music pulled her along; she played for almost an hour.

She went outside, leaving a light in the lounge in case a guest wandered in to read. Outside, the small circular patch of lawn in front of the Inn was drenched in moonlight. It would be a fine night in her white garden. Local gardeners found her shade gardens odd, the white garden oddest of all. She had planted it after reading about Vita Sackville West's garden at Sissinghurst, a garden meant for moonlit viewing. Parker had wanted to take her to England on a garden tour, had booked passage to surprise her. But she could not leave the Inn; they did not go. She walked along the path beside the stream to the garden. Beneath the full moon the palette of white on white was luminous — unearthly clouds of white phlox, silver leaves of artemisia, ghostly fern fronds. She inhaled the bitter perfume of achillea and then continued toward the lake. Moonlight seeped through the hemlock canopy. The scent of cigar hung in the air; she would find him soon.

She stepped into the clearing. The lake gleamed like a fallen moon. She noticed a canoe tethered by the floating dock before she saw him. Before she saw them. Every detail of the tableau was crisp and clear in the moonlight — the white waitress uniform was raked up under Carol's arms, the white panties crumpled at her ankles, his white buttocks were cradled between her long, muscular legs. His familiar moan of pleasure at climax wafted across the water. She walked to the water's edge and cleared her throat. The sound echoed. He rolled over and looked toward shore. She turned and walked away, chilly and short of breath. It seemed a long way, back to the Inn. She went behind the reception desk and selected a key for an empty guest room. She spent the night there, with the door locked from the inside. She heard him walk softly down the corridor. He had checked the guest register and found which key was missing and unaccounted for, determined the room she had chosen. He knocked at her locked door. She buried her head under the soft down pillows; it was fortunate she had been so careful to have thick pillows on every bed.

He left the Inn the next day. She did not have an opportunity to dismiss the waitress since Carol did not return. She knew the locals talked. The ache of grief and the burn of humiliation were entwined; she could not say which was more bitter.

She treated him with professional courtesy on his rare visits. They reviewed the Inn's accounts, agreed upon major expenses and repairs. It was easy to avoid sharing a bed with so many rooms, but it was hard to sleep alone, when he was there, under the same roof. The hunger of abstinence gnawed at her on those grim nights. She touched herself and found cold comfort. She remembered how he used to ask, voice crackling over the long distance wire, *Do you miss me, or the idea of me?* She touched herself and missed him, the flesh and blood of him between her legs.

There was no need to divorce. He stayed in the apartment in Pittsburgh, when he was not on the road. In the middle of the night three years ago a woman had telephoned from his apartment. He had been taken to the hospital with the stroke that would carry him off.

After that summer, after their unspoken separation, it was never the same at the Inn. Perhaps it was the building of the Turnpike, the war, but she suspected guests found the place too quiet, found her austere. One summer she invited musicians from Pittsburgh to stay as her guests, in exchange for house concerts. She hoped to attract professors from the University and placed discreet advertisements for "Chautauqua on the Juniata." Only a few came and she did not try again. Last year, years too late, *Yankee Magazine* discovered the Inn.

"A living museum of another time, the time of leisure and rest cures in long rambling wooden hotels."

After the article ran she had so many reservations for foliage season she opened and heated the guest rooms upstairs for the first time in years. The visitors disturbed her rooms, tramped off the trails and broke the laurel. She was relieved when the trees were bare and the "leaf peepers" gone. She was too old for success. The strenuous autumn was followed by a hard winter of deep snow. Her constant care and attention could not prevent gutters freezing, trees falling, the roof leaking. She remembered a huge Ming vase she had seen in the Carnegie. It had been unearthed in shards, painstakingly restored and cobbled together. Its surface was hatched with a tracery of repair lines, its beauty magnified by the evidence of the loving effort taken to mend it. The Inn had been her Ming vase but she was tired now. This spring his offer came and she accepted. She would move to Pittsburgh, back to the apartment and a subscription to the symphony. She would make a clean break from worry.

"More bubbly?" he asked.

"Thank you."

"I might thin out the trees, put in a little road out here, and campsites, for the family crowd."

She took a wafer of melba toast from the basket and sucked the corner until the crisp dry bread grew sweet and soft; she swallowed. Her head ached from the champagne.

"We should get back now. I must see to dinner."

They walked through evening shade. The stream splashed at the bottom of the gully beside the path.

"It's dark in here," he said.

"Hemlock makes deep shade."

She thought of the shelf of nature books in the lounge: *Ferns of North America, Trees of the Northeast, A Field Guide to Wildflowers.* She would leave them behind, she would not need them in Schenley Park or the Conservatory; city trees and plants wear labels. Would camping families leaf through her references, as they waited in the lounge before dinner in the dining room the last night of their stay, having dumped the melted ice from the coolers?

The lights of the Inn were ahead now. The long glowing façade stretched beside the road. There were no lights upstairs, no overnight guests. They climbed the steps. She felt the familiar, nightly flutter of worry. Who would come? When? Too many? Too early? Too late?

She heard voices from the lounge, Judge Clark and his wife, one

126

of the few local families who appreciated what she offered. They had come out from town, at least once a week, for years. She would not introduce him to the Clarks. She would seat him first, and then bring them in. The long rays of the evening sun slanted into the dining room. She memorized soft gray walls, the glow of pewter, crisp white linen, glinting crystal and silver. She seated him.

"Enjoy your meal. Lamb, with gravy or mint sauce, or brook trout this evening. With brussels sprouts, I like to call them cabbages disappointed in love." She made her husband's joke for the last time, and her guest laughed. She pushed through the swinging door into the kitchen.

"Ready? It is time," she said to Annie.

The girl hurried past her into the dining room. She stood for a moment by the round window in the swinging door and watched the little waitress in her snug white uniform cross the room to his table. Annie stood, poised to take his order. He looked up, and smiled. She recognized his proprietary glance. For a moment she wanted to summon the girl back to the kitchen, to pick up the phone and tell her young husband to come and take his wife away from this cove, back up the mountain. Well, it wasn't her affair. At least the girl would keep her job. She prepared her smile and went to usher the Clarks to dinner.

The end of the evening came; the dinner guests were gone. The buyer had lingered in the dining room and then spent a long time down in the game room. She found him now in the lounge, making notes.

"Those walls downstairs are thick," he said.

"Yes, it's a stone foundation."

"I'll get an electrician in. I'd like some pin ball machines down there for the kids."

"You'll need an electrician. The wiring is old."

She did not say that even a guest's hair drier could blow a fuse. Let him discover that.

Let the stout walls, the frail wires, slow him down.

"See you tomorrow at the closing," he said.

"Yes, at the closing."

He sprang down the steps and into his car. The engine roared and he sped away, gravel spitting from beneath his tires.

She walked back inside and paused in the lounge. His red roses stood on the piano, shining like neon in the dim room. She picked up the vase and carried it into the dining room. Annie had already blown out the candles and stripped the tables.

"Annie, here, take these home with you."

"Oh, ma'am, they are beautiful."

A horn sounded.

"That's my husband," said the girl.

"Go along then."

Priscilla walked back into the dining room. The laurel blossoms in the vase on the sideboard gleamed, white bells among deep green leaves. She reached out and touched the glossy foliage and remembered Parker stroking the marble Daphne a lifetime ago. What was Apollo's expression as he lost Daphne, as she escaped into another form?

She lifted the heavy vase and carried it outside and across to the springhouse. She knelt and placed it on the floor, then gathered the laurel in her hands and pulled it from the vase. Priscilla laid the dark leaves on the damp stones beside the spring, like an offering in a shrine, a tribute on a grave.

Idlewild

My grandfather died before I was born. Papa got the fishing cabin and Uncle Rob got the farm. "I got the best of the deal," my father said, though he had to go out of state to work, all the way to the oil rigs on the Gulf of Mexico.

My mother said we could get by if he stayed. "You're just restless. You don't even want to try."

"Annie, why be someone's hired hand for peanuts when I can make good money down there?"

Summers, he came home and we lived in the cabin: one big room with a little bedroom off the back. My parents had the bedroom and I slept on the sofa in the big room. There was no electricity, just lamplight. I liked the smell of lamp oil, and watching the soft shadows as I fell asleep. The cabin didn't have heat, so after my father went back to Texas, when school started, we moved to the trailer on Uncle Rob's farm. We didn't have any other family except my mother's father who lived alone on his farm. He hadn't talked to my mother since she got married. Sometimes we saw him in Don's Hardware. He had a tangled beard and old-fashioned clothes, like the Mennonites, but he wasn't one. My mother heard he wasn't welcome in any church in the valley anymore, because he tried to run things.

Mama was the prettiest, youngest mother in my class. People meeting us were surprised: she was strawberry blond, and I dark — like my father. That summer I was thirteen, only three years younger than she'd been when she had me. I'd gotten my monthly for the first time in the spring.

"Sarah, you're a woman now. You can have babies. Don't let the boys touch you, if you want to grow up to be a bride with a church wedding," she said, almost like she was mad at me. I had let a boy hold my hand on the school bus, but after what she said, I tried to sit alone.

My mother worked at the Inn, waitressing and housekeeping. All summer Papa and I drove her there by seven, for breakfast. We pulled up in front; they leaned together over my head and kissed. She'd climb out of the truck and pause beside his window for one more kiss. Then, "Be good you two," she'd say.

"Be good yourself, Annie," he replied.

She waved and disappeared around the back of the old white Inn.

We drove back to the cabin to fish for breakfast. My father liked to cook outdoors and he said, "I like fish any way you can catch them, any way you can cook them, any time you can eat them." He taught me how to make a roll cast. Watching the loop of line unfurl, he said I was a natural, and promised I would be a natural at hunting, too. But during hunting season he was never around to teach me.

After breakfast, we might take the canoe and go exploring down Ray's Branch. We saw an eagle once. Or he worked on projects — he put a new roof on the cabin that summer. I helped, or took my book and sat by the river to read. Thursdays, the Bookmobile came to the village and I could get new books; biographies were my favorite. The Bookmobile lady would pick out something for my mother, too. She knew Mama liked romance stories.

Afternoons, we drove to the lake: man-made but snug in the bowl between the hills as though it had always been there. Hiking trails crisscrossed through the hemlock woods. The north side of the lake was wild with steep cliffs, the south side a soft slope with campground, boat launch, and swimming beach. You could rent paddleboats but my father said they were for city people. The park rangers stocked the lake with bass. Some local fishermen came; my father called lake fishing too tame to bother with.

We'd walk through the picnic grove to the swimming beach. The biggest picnic shelter, the pavilion, could be reserved for family re-unions. Families came with coolers and grills and guitars and playpens. They hung crepe paper streamers and covered the tables with paper cloths and jello salads and giant bags of chips. The air was full of the noise of volleyball and badminton and sweet smoke from grilling meat. One family played a relay race: tying each other up in toilet paper, spray-ing Reddi-whip into open mouths. Sometimes the pavilion stood empty, and the sign said "Available." My family — us, a grandfather we didn't speak to, Uncle Rob and Aunt Lida — couldn't fill even the smallest shelter.

The swimming beach was grassy and shaded by oak trees, with a narrow strip of sand right by the water, trucked in each spring. We waded in the lake, startling clouds of little minnows, and swam out to the floating dock so Papa could dive. I liked to lie on my belly on the cool wet float, looking into the green water for shadows of big bass swimming down deep. That summer when I stretched out on the float it was uncomfortable — my breasts were new and small, but finally big enough to get in the way. I looked back at the shore where boys splashed girls and little children dug in the sand. Mothers from the campground pulled over wagons full of towels and thermoses and sat chatting in the shade. Sometimes there would be another local family; I could tell by the father's tan — neck and forearms deep brown, shoulders and chest white. "A farmer's tan," my father said. He was walnut brown all over.

For dinner we went to the Frosty Bear Drive In. I had onion rings and a cheeseburger, a strawberry milkshake so thick and cold sipping it made my head ache. He usually had a shrimp basket; he missed the shrimp down on the Gulf, "big as baby sunfish." Teenagers hung out at the Frosty Bear. From the truck's cab, as though in a bird blind, we watched the girls and boys sitting on the hoods of cars, laughing, eating ice cream.

"See that pretty girl over there?" he'd say, nodding toward a girl in short shorts, surrounded by a group of boys. "That'll be you in a couple years, Sarah. You'll have them eating out of your hand. You'll be the Bedford County Fall Foliage Queen."

I liked to imagine being a Fall Foliage Princess, riding on the back of a convertible in the parade, holding a big bouquet of asters, waving at the crowd. The parade ends at the Courthouse, where my parents got married. The fathers wait there, all dressed up. Each Princess and her father climb up the steps together, each father kisses his Princess and then walks down the steps to wait and see who gets picked Queen. I liked to picture my parents down in the crowd, their proud faces turned up to me, waiting for the news.

Mama got off at eight. We waited out front to pick her up. The Inn shone like a giant lantern in the dusk, all the windows on the first floor glowing. Usually a few guests were rocking in the chairs on the long porch. We could hear the soft clink of someone pitching horseshoes across the road. The night before he left for Texas, my mother came around the corner of the Inn carrying a big bouquet of dark red roses. Handing me the flowers, she climbed in. They didn't look like garden roses; the stems were long and straight and had no thorns.

"What's the occasion?" he asked. "Where did those come from?"

"The new owner came tonight. Settlement's tomorrow. He gave these to Mrs. Crichton. I don't think she liked them. She gave them to me."

Mrs. Crichton was old, and she was selling the Inn. My mother worried she might lose her job. Papa said she'd have to go work at the Frosty Bear and fend off the teenage boys. He was teasing; the Frosty closes Labor Day.

"What's he like?" my father asked.

"I don't know, loaded, judging from his car and clothes."

"How old?"

"Younger than old lady Crichton," she laughed, slipping off her white waitress shoes and stretching her long legs in their smooth hose across me and into his lap, resting her feet right between his legs. He stopped asking questions and drove home with one hand on the wheel, the other rubbing her foot. I held the roses; the cab of the truck filled with their heavy smell.

Back at the cabin, we roasted marshmallows outside at the fire circle.

"Do you want blonde or brunette? Rare or well-done?" he asked.

I preferred blonde, puffy and light gold. My mother liked hers roasted longer: brunette, well-done. My father pulled her marshmallow off the stick, and held it to her lips; she nibbled it right from his hand and then sucked on his fingers.

"I like redheads, medium-rare," he said, making her laugh.

That night, after roasting marshmallows, we drove to the lake to watch the meteor shower. We spread an old chenille bedspread down by the water. Kissing, my parents missed most of the shooting stars. The sky looked big and far away; I started imagining giant bass crawling out of the lake. Finally, Papa said it was time to head home.

We stepped into the dark cabin, filled with the dense scent of those roses. He lit the lantern on the table just as she leaned over the bouquet to breathe the fragrance. In the soft light, sniffing those deep red flowers, she looked like the picture of Rose Red in the fairy tale book.

"I'm leaving early," he said.

I knew. He'd been fixing up his motorcycle, packing, all afternoon. She hated for him to make that long trip on the bike but we needed the truck to be able to get around while he was gone. He might be back by Christmas.

"Be good. I want to hear about straight A's on that report card. Take care of this pretty lady here. Keep an eye on her."

"Who keeps an eye on you?" she asked, not laughing.

I wanted to grab onto him and keep him there with us; I wanted it to stay that night forever, the three of us in the circle of lamplight in the cabin.

He kissed the top of my head and lit another lantern. Taking my mother's hand, he led her into the bedroom and shut the door. I blew out my lantern and lay down on the sofa. Behind closed eyes, I could see the long green tails of meteors streaking across the sky. When I opened my eyes it was morning; he was gone.

"It's time for us to go to work," she said, cross, though I was ready.

School did not start until after Labor Day, so I spent the rest of August at the Inn. The new owner, Mr. Redmond, had moved in. My mother did the housekeeping in his suite. She told me he had drawers full of the sweaters he wore on cool evenings, "cashmere, soft as a cloud." One day I sat at the kitchen table polishing silver, listening to my mother and the cook talk about the changes he was making.

"All these choices on the menu make my job harder," said the cook.

"It makes waitressing harder too, but set menus like Mrs. Crichton's are old fashioned. He'll attract more travelers from the turnpike this way."

"Maybe so," said the cook, "but Judge Clark isn't coming Sunday nights anymore."

"Well, some people just don't like change," Mama said.

"Mrs. Clark said something to me when I ran into her at the grocery."

"What?"

"Judge told her Redmond used to be a lawyer in Harrisburg but his family bought him this place to get him out of town."

"Why?"

"She wouldn't say. Maybe he had his hand in someone's till."

"With so much money of his own?"

"Maybe that's not it. I don't care one way or the other, so long as we stay open and I get paid."

We ate breakfast every day in the big kitchen, and then I helped set tables in the dining room. My mother showed me how to fold the linen napkins into swans. Afterwards, I liked to stand in the little passageway, the butler's pantry, between the kitchen and the dining room. It made a good hiding spot; I could look through the round porthole window in the swinging door to watch the guests eat breakfast and find out if there were any children.

Mr. Redmond visited the kitchen before his breakfast.

"Good morning, ladies. It smells delicious."

He brushed past me, smelling like pine needles, and sat at his table in the dining room by the west window. My mother brought his breakfast, always two poached eggs on English muffins, no matter what the cook was making.

"Thank you, Annie," he would say, looking up at her and smiling.

He was nicer than Mrs. Crichton had been. One morning when Mama put his plate down, her hand shook and one of the eggs

136

slipped into his lap. Turning red like she might cry, she picked up the linen napkin, dipped it in the tumbler of water, and held it out to him.

"I'm so sorry, sir. Quick, before the yolk sets."

"That's alright. Perhaps you could help."

She hesitated, and then stooped beside him, dabbing at the egg on his corduroy pants leg. He did not complain.

After breakfast and dining room set-up, my mother made beds. I could spend the whole day outside, so long as I checked in at lunchtime. I wandered in the hemlock forest surrounding the Inn, waded in the stream, and built stone and twig fairy houses. The bridle path led to the swimming pond: if guests were there, I could go in. Sometimes I brought my rod and tackle and went further, to the trout pool — just to catch and release, the fish were reserved for guests. I didn't go often; it wasn't the same as fishing in the river with my father. Rainy days, I read through the shelves of nature books and local history in the Lounge. I sat on the long porch in one of the dozens of rockers pulled up to the rocking rail. Rain drummed on the tin roof, the rocker creaked. If there were children staying, I might join them for ping-pong and shuffleboard in the basement game room.

My favorite place was the bowling alley in the wooden building across from the Inn. I liked to play by myself there, to set up the wooden pins, and send the heavy ball rumbling down the lane to crash them down. One day Mr. Redmond came in.

"Oh, Sarah, it's you. I heard the noise."

"I always set the pins and put the balls back before I leave."

"That's fine. All alone? Want me to be your pin boy?"

He walked to the end of the lane and set the pins. I rolled a strike.

"Good work," he said, setting the pins again.

We played for some time, taking turns bowling and setting.

"So you come every day with your mother?"

"Till school starts."

"Is it lonely?"

"Not really."

"I was on my way to the stables for a ride. Join me."

"I don't know how."

"I'll teach you. Let's tell your mother."

We walked back to the Inn and found her setting tables.

"Annie, I'm taking your daughter for a riding lesson. Just the easy trail out to the trout pool."

"She hasn't been around horses much."

"I'll enjoy showing her the ropes."

"Be careful," my mother said, looking at me with a worried frown.

"I'll take good care of her," he said.

She leaned over and hugged me. "Be careful," she whispered in my ear.

Crickets buzzed and helicoptered in the bright air as we walked along the path. The stable had been empty until Mr. Redmond came and brought four horses to the Inn, for the guests. The groundskeeper brought out the smallest horse for me, but she looked enormous. Mr. Redmond helped me up. His hand rested on the small of my back, steadying me, as he led me around the paddock.

"Sit easy and just hold the reins like this. Good."

We rode out to the trout pool. I began to relax into the rocking motion. After that, he gave me a riding lesson almost every afternoon. We rode farther and farther along the trails. He was learning his new property; I pretended we were explorers, pioneers. Every day I hated to arrive back at the stable, but looked forward to the moment when he held me close and lifted me down from the horse.

One day, walking back together from the stable, we discovered a dark green car, low and sleek, parked beside the Inn. A woman, in a blue sheath dress and a hat with a veil, sat rocking on the porch. He stood at the foot of the stairs, looking up at her. I hung back.

"Hello, Paul," she said.

"Hello."

"Is there a place we could talk?"

"Yes," he said and walked up onto the porch. He held the wide screen door open. "This way," he said, and showed her down the dark hall past the office to his private suite. He shut the door behind them.

In the kitchen, I poured myself a glass of lemonade. I found Mama and the cook sitting on the side steps, drinking iced tea and staring at the woman's car.

"Foreign. Italian," said the cook.

"Did he introduce you?" my mother asked me.

"No."

"Did you get a good look? Was she wearing a wedding ring?" asked the cook.

"I don't know. She was pretty."

"Well, looks like we have a guest for dinner tonight. And I lay odds she'll be here for breakfast, too, without you needing to make up another room, Annie."

My mother just sat dunking the stem of mint in and out of her tea.

The cook was wrong. Before I had even finished my lemonade, the woman hurried across the lawn to her car. Gravel spit out from under her wheels as she roared away.

That evening, he sat at his usual table as though nothing had happened. Mama brought him his soup.

"Join us on our ride tomorrow. See what a fine horsewoman your daughter is," he said.

"Thank you, sir, but I couldn't."

"By my decree. You can be excused from your other duties. We're not full."

The next morning he told the cook my mother had the afternoon off.

"Certainly," she said, raising her eyebrows.

After lunch, my mother came out to the stable in her jeans and checked blouse.

"I've never seen you out of uniform before, Annie. Very nice," he said.

She blushed.

"Let me help you up," he said, and boosted her into the saddle. "You're not much heavier than your daughter."

Not true: I weighed ninety-one pounds, she at least a hundred. He showed her how to sit and hold the reins. He walked beside her around the paddock, keeping his hand low on her back. Then he stood and watched her practice; she shot a glance at him each time she trotted past.

We rode out to the trout pool. He lifted her down, and then me, and we sat for a long time, not talking, just watching dragonflies — hooked to each other — skimming across the water.

One morning several days later, I hid in the pantry, keeping an eye on breakfast. Mr. Redmond sat at his table. Mama brought the coffee pot, turned his cup over, and poured.

"Good morning, Annie."

"Good morning, sir. I'll get your eggs."

"Just a moment," he said, reaching out and catching her wrist. "I want to take Sarah to Idlewild, sort of a last fling of summer. You too. Your day off is tomorrow, isn't it?"

Idlewild! The amusement park in the mountains. I held my breath, afraid she'd say no. We had already planned to spend her day off shopping the sales for school supplies and clothes. She'd said I should start wearing brassieres, and promised me a garter belt and nylons for dressing up, even though we had to be very careful about money. Now that summer was ending, she worried Mr. Redmond might not need her anymore and she would lose her job.

"Thank you, but we have Sarah's school shopping to do."

"I'd be disappointed," he said, still grasping her wrist. "You've worked hard all summer. Besides, I should get to know my employees better, when I'm thinking of keeping them on for the winter."

She stood very still. "Thank you. We'd be delighted," she said.

Mr. Redmond came to pick us up the next morning, driving his gray green car with the top down. He parked beside our truck; the pickup looked shabby next to the convertible.

"What a charming spot," he said, getting out and looking around.

"My husband and his father built it."

"That road must be tough in the winter."

"We rent a trailer from my brother-in-law, once school starts. There's no heat in here."

Walking up to the cabin door, he went in without waiting to be invited. He seemed to fill up the whole room.

"Well, isn't this rustic. I've thought I should have a couple of cabins out by the trout pool. Perhaps your husband could help."

"Yes, when he's back."

"And when will that be?" he asked, stepping toward her.

"It's hard for him to tell," she said, moving behind the table to clear our breakfast dishes away.

We always sat and read at breakfast, on our day off. He picked up my book first, *Cheaper by the Dozen*, then her paperback romance. The cover showed a man lifting a woman in a cape onto a horse.

"Perhaps we should get your mother a cloak, when the weather turns cold," he said to me.

A train used to run past the Inn to Idlewild, and then on to Pittsburgh. But we drove along Route 30 , the Lincoln Highway. The road follows the top of the mountains the whole way. I rode in the back seat of the convertible, pretending to be a Fall Foliage Princess, practicing my wave. Mama had tied a scarf over her head, but even so her red curls whipped and bounced as we rushed along. The car trip seemed more like flying than driving: almost as good as the wooden roller coaster, our first ride at Idlewild.

Mr. Redmond paid; all three of us squeezed on one seat, me in the middle. The roller coaster man locked us in and we rocketed away, up and down, brushing through the treetops, my mother and me screaming and closing our eyes. He wrapped his arms around us.

Afterward, we needed the peaceful Ferris wheel. We swayed for a while up at the very top, listening to hurdy-gurdy music from the carousel, and rattles and screams from the roller coaster hidden by the canopy of hemlock branches below. I sat between them again; his arms rested across our shoulders.

They waited for me while I rode the carousel. I waved every time I went by, on my white horse with the gold mane, but they didn't notice. The shoulder strap of her seersucker sundress had slipped; he fiddled with it.

He bought two cones of cotton candy and said he didn't want any, but kept stealing bites from hers.

After dark, we drove home. I stretched out in the back seat; my mother rested her head by Mr. Redmond's shoulder. The car's engine purred. Next thing I knew, he was carrying me into the cabin. Mama lit a lantern and led him to the bedroom where he laid me down. I fell back to sleep, listening to the murmur of their voices in the next room.

Idlewild marked the end of summer: we'd move to the trailer the next weekend. But Thursday, driving home from the Inn, she said, "I have good news."

My heart pounded. Maybe Papa was coming home early from the Gulf to build cabins at the Inn for Mr. Redmond.

"We don't have to move to the trailer! Mr. Redmond is keeping me on and says we can stay in the apartment over the bowling alley. No rent, and closer to school than Uncle Rob's." She sounded giddy.

I loved the apartment — like a tree house, with sloping ceilings and rough plank floors. We ate our meals in the kitchen at the Inn. No one brought children after school began. Our guests, retired couples, came for the foliage: "leaf peepers," we called them. Sometimes at dinner Mr. Redmond asked me to join him at his table and we had fun with Mama, giving her a hard time, sending her back and forth to the kitchen. After dinner, I did my homework in the lounge while she set up the dining room for breakfast. When I finished, I worked the jigsaw puzzle kept on a card table for guests. Often Mr. Redmond invited me down to the game room for ping-pong. Mama came after she finished, and we teamed up against him. If my father had been there, Mr. Redmond and I could have played against my parents. Once I hit the ball so hard it ricocheted off the beam in the low ceiling and made him laugh. Afterwards, I tried to hit it wild on purpose, to hear his laugh. A fire burned on the big stone hearth; the basement room — damp and cool all summer — now felt like a warm cave. We'd finish ping-pong and sit in rocking chairs around the fireplace, staring into the flames. Until she said,

"School night. Time for bed, Sarah."

"Let me escort you ladies home, protect you from the wolves."

"No, thanks," she said.

"I won't take no for an answer."

He came upstairs: so tall his head brushed the rafters. I listened to their voices rise and fall until I fell asleep.

One morning, I missed the school bus and dawdled back to the Inn, dreading telling my mother. She would be angry at having to take me to school, and the cook (who didn't like us much anymore) would be angry with her. I found Mama setting tables in the dining room; Mr. Redmond sat in his usual spot, watching her. They both looked up as I came in.

"Not again, Sarah. Why can't you pack your satchel the night before?" she said.

"I'm sorry. The bus came early."

"I'll take her," he said.

"Oh no," said my mother, untying her apron, "I couldn't impose on you."

"It's no trouble, Annie," he said, "Besides, I need you here. There's a lot to do with that tour group coming in tonight."

So I rode to school in the convertible. Too cold that day to have the top down, but I hoped some of my classmates looked out and saw me swoop up like Cinderella in the coach.

Not long after, I missed the bus again and trudged along the road to the Inn, my satchel banging against my hip. I knew Mama was very busy; we'd had a full house the night before and another leaf peeper tour on the way. Mrs. Crichton had never let tour groups stay. The cook complained about the extra work.

"He's a good businessman, and not a snob," Mama said.

"You'd be the one to know," the cook said.

I crept in the front door, avoiding the kitchen and the cook. If I encountered Mr. Redmond first, maybe he'd offer to take me. I found the dining room empty. My mother would be changing beds in the guest rooms upstairs; perhaps she'd let me play hooky and help. I hated picking up the damp, used towels but enjoyed snapping heavy clean sheets in the air above the beds, my mother holding the opposite side.

Upstairs, on housekeeping mornings, the guest room doors hung open, letting light pour into the hallway. I peeked into each room as I passed: every bed in the Inn was different, antiques Mrs. Crichton had collected. The beds were stripped, fresh linens lay folded, waiting. The door to the last guest room (the one with my favorite bed, the sleigh bed) was closed; I hesitated, and then pushed it open.

Sunlight reflected off the glossy pine floor and flooded the room with warm honey colored light — so bright I blinked. In the half-made bed, amidst a tousle of sheets and blankets, my mother and Mr. Redmond lay tangled together. She saw me first; he rolled over. They sat up.

"What are you doing here?" she asked, patting her mussed hair.

"The bus came early again."

"Go downstairs. I'll be right there."

I waited in the lounge. Her footsteps sounded on the stairs and down the hall.

"Let's go, Sarah."

Without a word, I followed her out to the truck. We drove all the way to school in silence. I turned away when she leaned across the seat to kiss me.

After school, I didn't go to the Inn kitchen to snack and visit with my mother as usual. I marched into the bowling alley and hurled the ball: it rumbled and thundered down the lane, crashing into the pins. Mr. Redmond came in.

"I'll be your pin boy," he said, walking down the lane and stooping to set the pins. He rolled the ball back down the raised wooden gutter. "Ready when you are," he said.

I turned away and headed for the stairs to our apartment.

"They've asked me to drive one of the princesses in the parade. Ride with me. Great publicity for the Inn, pretty girl like you."

"Take my mother," I muttered under my breath, but loud enough.

He caught up with me, grabbed my shoulders and yanked me around. We stood so close I could smell him, spicy as a Christmas tree. I remembered how he lifted me from the horse and held me mid-air, how he carried me from car to bed, after Idlewild.

"I am taking your mother."

"My father wouldn't like it."

"Too bad he's not here. He could come too." He smiled; his teeth were very white.

"I'll ride with you. But only if she doesn't," I said, staring right in his eyes: gray green, like his convertible.

"Well, well," he said.

He had me backed up against the wall. I felt dizzy and hollowed out, like the moment just past the very top of the roller coaster. I kissed him on the mouth.

My mother came in.

"I was just telling Sarah about the parade," he said, stepping away.

She looked at him, and then at me, and then at him again. He left. My mother stared after him.

"Get upstairs and don't come down. I'll bring your dinner over," she said, pushing me to the steps.

She brought me a tray with fried chicken and gravy and mashed potatoes but I wasn't hungry. I sat by my window, looking across to the lighted dining room, watching his silhouette at the window table.

We moved to the trailer the next day.

Neither of us rode in the parade, when the time came. My mother did not even go, working her new job over at the Howard Johnson's on the turnpike. But I went, with my aunt and uncle. We found a good spot to watch.

145

He drove by in his gray green convertible, beeping the car horn. No one rode beside him on the soft leather seat, but the prettiest princess in the whole parade — the one from Chestnut Ridge — perched on the back of his car, waving her wave. We skipped the coronation at the courthouse; I did not see the princesses and their fathers climb the steps together.

His picture appeared in *The Gazette.* Grinning beneath sunglasses like a movie star; driving his princess, the chosen Queen. My mother snatched the page away. She stood by the sink, studying the photo, then glanced at me and dumped the coffee grounds right on his face.

Later, I fished the paper from the trash.

Dance Lessons

Clarice had fallen and broken her hip last winter. She was lucky, her daughter Lucy said, that it was the cleaning lady's day or she might have lain undiscovered. Clarice's only memory of the fall was fear and pain, her only recollection of the hospital was ringing for pain medicine and waiting. The sharp pain was gone now, replaced by the dull ache of boredom. According to Lucy, the doctors had insisted she could not live alone, she needed care and rehabilitation and to be near family.

"And you must be careful, you have osteoporosis, bones like graham crackers, the doctors said," Lucy told her.

Her son-in-law, a lawyer, said she could not afford to keep her apartment in Pittsburgh nor the cost of care in the city. Clarice did not recall agreeing to move near her daughter, but now here she was, almost eighty, stranded in a small town rest home among dozens of old women and a few old men.

"Rest home is a ridiculous euphemism," she told her daughter. "Are we resting from life? Resting up for death?"

"Don't be dramatic, Mother," said Lucy.

Clarice awoke in the middle of every long night, needing the bathroom, forgetting where she was until — struggling to get up — she encountered the bedside railing.

"I don't appreciate being a prisoner here," she told her daughter who stopped in every day on her way home from work at the library.

"Oh, hush," Lucy said. "Look how pretty your room is, with your pictures on the wall, the plants on the window sill."

The rest home, like its residents and like the town, had seen better, livelier days. Tourists used to be drawn to the area by mineral springs. Years ago, Clarice and her second husband had attended conventions at The Springs, the big resort hotel just outside of town. It had been pleasant, dancing, golfing, soaking in the baths. Lucy had recently taken her to lunch at The Springs. It was shabby and rundown now.

The more modest hotels in town had closed altogether or, like this one, been converted to other use.

Her room looked like what it was, a drab hotel room hybridized into a hospital cell. The plants and pictures were only window dressing. The aluminum contraption she had used to learn to walk again leaned in one corner. Clarice had "graduated" to a four-pronged cane but refused to use it. She detested the practical sneakers with velcro closures; the staff made her wear "running shoes" although she could barely walk. Her room was on the fourth floor and looked out over the little river that ran through town. She could open the window and hurl herself out, if she had the strength, if she did not want the shame of her obituary reading that she had died here. W.C. Fields would have said that it was redundant to die in this town.

"Up and at 'em, Clarice, it's bingo time," said the plump woman, bursting into the room without knocking. *Activities Director* said her name tag, as though this were some pleasure cruise.

"Not today."

"We'll miss you. Your boyfriends will be asking for you!"

Clarice thought that unlikely. The few men here barely spoke.

"Well, don't mope in the dark," the woman said, whipping up the venetian blinds and snapping on the fluorescent light.

"Turn that off."

"Just trying to brighten up your day."

She bustled out. Clarice knew she had hurt her feelings. Lucy warned her about "alienating the staff" and wooed them with offerings of candy and flowers. Clarice had never been good with women; they bored her. When she was young, before she married, she enjoyed her job as a bank teller. She dressed in tight straight skirts, silky blouses, high heels. A line of men waited at her window, even when there was no queue for other tellers. She cashed their checks and dispensed crisp bills like manna from her manicured fingers. Lunch hours she took dancing classes and spun through the studio in the teacher's arms, charmed, enchanted by her own reflection in the mirrored walls. She waltzed back to the bank with the music in her ears.

She should have asked that silly woman to turn on the music.

She could not seem to learn, or remember, how to operate the machine Lucy had brought when Clarice complained that there was no classical music on the radio here. She was probably the only person in this place who had ever been to an opera. Now she had a mute pile of silvery disks and a mysterious machine.

The phone on her bed stand rang. No one called from the outside world except Lucy, her daughter, jailer, lifeline. She remembered, although she did not like to, the letters Lucy had written from boarding school. Clarice had tucked the girl away so she could travel with her new husband and have a little fun after the hard years as a young widow, a single mother. Lucy had pleaded to come home. She let the phone ring.

The charge nurse came into her room. The warden, Clarice called her when speaking to Lucy.

"Stop that. She's taking very good care of you. You look a world better than that first day I saw you in the hospital."

"I wish I had died on my own floor," Clarice would reply, not entirely sure she meant it but liking her power to evoke fear in Lucy's pale blue eyes.

Now the nurse said, "Time for lunch. Have you been walking?"

"Not yet."

"You know what the physical therapist said. You've got to walk."

Of course she knew what David said. She remembered his every word. He was young, and handsome.

"Stand straight, Clarice. I won't let you fall," he had said as he reached his hands under her arms and pulled her up from the bed. His strong arms had supported her first halting attempts to walk; it had been a long time since a man held her. Now he did not come anymore.

"You don't need more therapy," Lucy had explained. "The insurance won't pay for it. Now you just need to practice walking by yourself."

The nurse waited at the door of her room.

"Come along, dear."

"Let me put my lipstick on," said Clarice.

She hoped the woman would leave, go down the hall to bother someone else.

"You don't want your soup to get cold, Clarice."

Hot or cold, the soup would be bland. She made awkward progress down the hallway, leaning on the handrail on the wall since no one was watching. The dining room smelled of overripe fruit and rancid steam from the dishwasher in the kitchen. How could anyone eat in this atmosphere? The room was festooned with limp crepe paper streamers, red construction-paper hearts, as though for a children's party.

"Like the decorations?" asked the activities director. "It's our annual Valentines Prom on Friday. The kids from the high school come, and all the staff. You'll love it. Bet you'll be the belle of the ball and have a full dance card."

Clarice straightened in her chair. A dance. David, the physical therapist, would be there. She felt like a racehorse in the starting gate. What would she wear? After lunch she called Lucy.

"I must have my hair done. And I need to come to your house to look at my clothes." Here she had only the knit sweat suits Lucy had purchased for her rehabilitation.

"Mother, what's going on?"

"There's a dance Friday. And get me one of those disc things of dance music. Waltzes, rumba, some cha-cha."

Thursday afternoon Lucy parked in a handicapped space behind Andrea's Styling Salon. The rough asphalt parking lot frightened Clarice but she would never be seen in public leaning on a cane. She had intentionally left hers behind in the car. She was relieved to reach the shop. It was small town and old-fashioned but she breathed in the caustic perfume of permanent wave lotion and nail polish and recognized the fragrant promise of transformation.

The stylist, plump and sympathetic, ran a comb through Clarice's thin hair. It had been months since a cut and color. Before the accident she had never missed the weekly appointment with her hairdresser in Pittsburgh.

"So, what do you want to do, dear?"

"I need a cut, not too short, and a wave. And color. Strawberry blonde."

"Are you sure, Mother? Strawberry blonde is awfully youthful."

"It's my color and it's my hair."

"Up to you," said Lucy.

"One make-over, coming up," said the stylist.

"I'll go run some errands," said Lucy. The bell rang over the door as she left.

Clarice navigated the length of the shop to the wash station. She almost fell into the chair; it was too low. She leaned back. Warm water rushed over her scalp, strong fingers sudsed and massaged. She closed her eyes. After the shampoo Clarice could not get up from the low-slung chair. The stylist hoisted her and helped her to the cutting station. Clarice looked away from her reflection. Thin wet hair slicked to her skull, she looked cadaverous.

"Okay, dear, let's get going. How short did you have in mind?"

The familiar questions, the gentle tug of the comb through wet hair, encouraged her.

"Not too short, but it needs shape."

The scissors clicked and snipped and wet fronds of hair fell to the floor. Clarice entered into the customary rite. She would be made new; she would be reborn.

Cut and colored, she sat beneath the beehive drier, baking in her permanent wave. She closed her eyes, lulled by the heat and roar of dry air. She was flying across a dance floor in the flourish and swirl of a Viennese waltz.

"Rise and shine, time to rinse and comb you out," said the stylist.

She pruned and pouffed Clarice's hair, misted it with spray, and gave her a hand mirror. She spun the chair while Clarice studied herself from every angle. The ritual had worked the customary miracle. She looked alive again beneath the cloud of bright hair.

"Well, if you don't mind my saying so, you look years younger," said the stylist.

The girl had earned a nice tip. Clarice, humiliated, remembered she was an inmate of an institution with neither checks nor cash in her handbag, nothing but a lipstick and a tissue. Lucy would have to pay.

"Here I am, Mother," said Lucy as she pushed through the door. "Goodness, we should have taken 'before and after' pictures!"

They drove back to Lucy's. The big stone house stood on a street of fine homes, souvenirs of the town's lost elegance. They ate dinner alone; Lucy said her husband was working late. Clarice could not imagine what kept a small town lawyer so busy and suspected he wanted to avoid her.

The jewel tones of Clarice's own carpet glowed on Lucy's dining room floor, and Clarice's crystal glinted in her daughter's china cupboard. Lucy had been quick to appropriate the best and most beautiful possessions from the apartment. "Better for your things to be used than sold, Mother. And there's no point in storing them," her practical daughter had said. True, Clarice had no use for carpets and crystal in her little cell but she wanted them back. She wanted her life back.

"What do you want to wear to the dance? I'll bring it down," Lucy said after they finished eating.

"I'll go look."

"Don't risk the stairs, Mother."

She ignored her daughter and began to climb, grasping the banister like a belaying rope. Lucy hovered behind her.

"Be careful. Don't fall."

"Stop making me nervous."

Clarice trembled with effort and fear. She gained the landing, and then achieved the upstairs hall.

"You did it, Mother!"

"It's just a flight of stairs, don't make such a fuss," said Clarice, more relieved than triumphant.

She went into the spare room and opened the wardrobe, fragrant with cedar and mothballs, filled with her gowns. Flipping through the hangers was like turning satin pages in a scrapbook. She remembered what it was to be the most charming woman in the room, in exactly the right dress. There was magic in silk and lace. Once again, in the right gown she would become an enchantress. Clarice selected the green shantung.

"Isn't it rather flashy?" Lucy asked.

Clarice did not bother to respond.

"Well, at least try it on. See if it fits."

"Of course it fits. It was made for me. Where are my shoes?"

"You're not wearing heels. You'd break your neck."

"Just to look."

Lucy knelt and pulled shoeboxes from under the bed. Clarice opened boxes until she came to her green beaded pumps.

"I'll take these, just for decoration in my room, a memento."

Lucy preceded her downstairs, carrying the dress and shoes.

"Careful, Mother."

Clarice was too frightened by the steep descent to reply. She took one stair at a time, gripping the banister white-knuckled. Her hip grated as she moved.

She was so tired it was almost good to arrive back at the rest home. The evening receptionist looked up from her magazine.

"You've had your hair done!"

Her daughter hung the dress in the closet. It gleamed among the knit jersey sweat suits. Lucy put the green pumps on the windowsill.

"How did you ever walk in those, let alone dance? Oh — I nearly forgot," she said, fishing in her handbag. "I found a CD for you. A medley of dance tunes."

Lucy put it in the machine. Bright notes spun into the air.

"Rest up for tomorrow."

Her daughter lingered a moment before leaving. Clarice realized after she was gone that Lucy had waited to be thanked, for the outing. She had never been good with Lucy, perhaps she would have done better with a son. She could telephone her now, but the excitement of the day had drained her. She was too weary. The aide came and helped her into bed. It was good to rest her head on the pillow, though she hoped she would not crush her curls. Clarice fell asleep listening to a cha-cha.

"Good morning," said the aide as she rattled open the venetian blinds.

Sunlight flooded the room. Clarice lay in bed. Her green beaded shoes sparkled on the windowsill. Today was the dance. It had been a long time since she awakened with this bubble of anticipation.

"Time for your shower."

"Not today. I can't get my hair wet. Do you know how to turn on this machine? I want to listen to my music."

She stayed in her room all day, refusing bingo and current events and chair exercise. She learned to press the *Play* button when the disc stopped and start the music again. As the dance music played she rehearsed steps and turns in her mind; she closed her eyes and flew across polished floors in mirrored rooms.

The evening aide helped her into the green gown before dinner.

"Wow, this is some dress, Clarice. What's it made of?"

"Raw silk. Shantung. From China."

In the dining room her iridescent green stood out like a beacon among the muddy pink and lavender knits the others wore — grandmother of the bride dresses. She remembered her first husband whispering in her ear at a dull faculty party, *You are like a bird of paradise among the wrens.* She hid her sneakers beneath the table.

"Look, Clarice! We have flowers," said one of her tablemates, one of the few who could converse, not that the woman had anything to say. There was a carnation corsage by each place. The activities director circulated, pinning on the flowers. Clarice looked down at the white blossom on her shoulder strap; she preferred gardenias.

After dinner she stood by the window in her room and stroked the green shoes. She could wear them; she would be leaning into the arms of a strong young partner. Clarice sat on the edge of her bed. Since the accident she had not put on shoes by herself. She did not ring for help, the foolish aide would never let her wear the heels. She pushed the sneakers off with her feet. Then she leaned over and almost somersaulted to the floor as she pulled off her socks. Dizzy and exhausted she lay back on the pillows. It was time for the dance. She sat up and slipped on the green shoes, admiring her narrow, high arched feet.

Clarice teetered down the hall, grabbing the wall rail. Tonight the floor seemed uneven, shifting beneath her feet as though she were on a cruise ship after all, heaving through rough sea. She made it to the dining room. The tables had been pushed into one corner. A mirrored ball spun from the chandelier. The lights were too bright. A fox trot played on what the activity director called her "boom box." Boys from the high school huddled at the punch bowl. Girls in short dresses and spike heels clustered together like bright bouquets. The residents slumped on chairs around the edge of the floor. Clarice looked for David, but her physical therapist was not there yet. The activities director picked up a microphone.

"Welcome, welcome to our Valentines Prom. Girls, boys, find a partner and have a lovely evening."

The girls, giggling, fanned out across the room. Soon the few frail gentlemen were claimed and shuffled around the floor, leaning on their slender partners. The activities director pushed the boys away from the punch table.

"Go, go, don't be bashful."

Elderly women outnumbered the boys. No one chose Clarice. She sat and watched mismatched couples make tentative, ungraceful progress around the floor. The young people did not know the steps, the old people could no longer execute them. What was she doing here?

She would go powder her nose. David would be here soon, then she and the physical therapist would show them how to dance. Clarice pushed herself to stand, almost losing her balance, twisting her ankle in the green shoes. She leaned against the wall and limped to the restroom. Might as well go, she thought, entering the handicapped stall and latching the door. She hoisted her dress, pulled down her panties, and lowered herself to the seat, gripping the grab bar with one hand, irritated that peeing was such a production.

Quick footsteps sounded on the tiles. Some girls had come to primp.

"Borrow your lip gloss? Thanks."

"Can you believe this?"

"I know. Fright's night out!"

157

"Well, we get the community service credits."

So this was not a dance. This was a charity event.

"How about the one in green?"

"Hair like cotton candy!"

"Is my slip showing?"

Feet clicked out and silence fell. Clarice sat. The toilet seat was cold and her hip ached. She pulled herself up with the grab rail and left the stall. She washed her hands, leaning against the sink, and looked at her reflection in the mirror. So this was what the girls saw. Frizzy hair, scalp like a hard boiled egg showing through, face wrinkled as tissue paper. The gown was too big, the bodice gaped over her shrunken bust. The corsage pulled the strap of her dress askew and the edges of the limp white carnation were already turning brown. Clarice unpinned the flower and threw it in the trash.

She wished to retreat to her room but did not trust herself to make it down the hall without falling. Clarice wobbled back into the dining room and collapsed onto a chair near the door. The music was loud.

"Now that's what I call a dress," said a dry, wavering voice. "Raw silk, isn't it?"

She turned. It was the man in the wheelchair who sometimes came to Bingo.

He was wearing a white linen dinner jacket, well tailored, though a little too large. His red bow tie was crisp and elegant.

Just then one of the boys came and stood before her.

"Would you care to dance, ma'am?"

Clarice looked up at him. His awkward, slender wrists dangled from the too-short cuffs of a blue polyester blazer.

"Thank you, no. I seem to have worn the wrong shoes."

The man in the wheel chair leaned forward to look down at her feet.

"I think you are wearing just the right shoes," he said, smiling.

She felt a familiar tingle. There would be no more dancing, but she could still practice the art of flirtation. Clarice tilted her head and smiled back.

158

Artesian Springs

All afternoon Grace and her daughter had waded deep into the blackberry thickets, armored in heavy overalls and work boots against the fierce thorns, lurking snakes, and poison ivy. Sweat dripped down Grace's back. A grasshopper, drunk with heat, cruised through the air and landed in her hair.

"Let's call it a day. We have enough," she said to Kate over the chirring rasp of the katydids and crickets.

Grace and Alan had bought the old farm six years ago, for the views. She had grown up spending summers on her grandparents' farm in Missouri, and wanted that for her children. Alan had indulged her. The house, the original chestnut logs sheathed in clapboard, perched on the crest of a ridge. You could look north from the porch down the meadow and out over the dark green forest to the receding, repeating blue Alleghenies or east to Will's Knob where at night the tiny red eye of the fire tower blinked. The farm had been in the same family for a hundred years until they came.

The first summers, they reveled in the space and quiet, so different from their city home in Pittsburgh. Alan wrote while she reclaimed the peonies, roses, and lilacs from years of neglect and a tide of honeysuckle. Their two daughters spent hours in the woods and creek. At night, after the girls were asleep, she and Alan spread an old quilt on the lawn and lay together, watching fireflies and shooting stars, making love with appetite forgotten since they had children. And then they went inside to bed, curled up together beneath the carved oak headboard of the antique bed that had come with the house, and fell into deep sleep. Those summers seemed a long time ago, now.

Last summer their eldest daughter, Frances, had turned fifteen and a flood of hormones invaded her. She was restless and bored, pined for her friends in the city, picked fights with Kate, mooned over the boy from the farm down the road. So this year they had sent her to camp with her best friend. Alan had remained in town, teaching summer school, and joined Grace and Kate at the farm on weekends. Grace had

161

both wanted the respite of separation and hesitated to leave him alone, and he knew it.

"It's over. I won't see her, I promise," he had whispered across the bed on her last night in Pittsburgh. "What will it take for you to believe me?"

"I don't know," she had said and rolled away. She still did not know.

Now, hot, itchy, Grace and Kate pushed out of the brambles and walked back to the house. At the back steps, hidden from the road, they stripped to panties and bras.

Whispers of breeze blew up the hillside and evaporated the sweat. A wasp buzzed over the buckets of sweet fruit. Grace would make jars of preserves, and freeze some fruit for cobblers and pie. She loved a kitchen fragrant with the steam of cooking fruit; it brought back the childhood summers on her grandmother's farm in Missouri.

"I wish we had an outdoor shower here, like at a beach house," said Kate. The farmhouse was so old that indoor plumbing had not been added until years after it was built. The unused outhouse still stood behind the lilac hedge in a far corner of the yard. The biggest upstairs bedroom had been converted to a bathroom decades back when running water was piped inside. The best view in the house was to be had from the old claw-foot tub, but there was no shower.

"You can use my bath oil," said Grace. Luxurious sandalwood, a conciliatory offering from Alan. She could not yet bring herself to use it.

"Thanks!" said Kate, running upstairs. Grace heard the bathroom door slam. The girl had become modest and private, hiding the body Grace used to know as well as she knew her own. Grace imagined her now, deep in the tub, warm water lapping over her sharp hipbones, her small, perfect breasts. Kate would soon be in full thrall to adolescence. Already at home in Pittsburgh she took long showers, letting the water run until her father called through the door, "Turn it off!" Already she slept late, the drugged sleep of young bodies in metamorphosis. There was a current of change eddying through the family, a contagious restlessness that had caught Alan, too.

Grace took her turn bathing after Kate finished. She inhaled the residual sandalwood steam from her daughter's long bath. Even second hand it was a beautiful fragrance. She toweled dry and inventoried her reflection in the full-length mirror on the back of the bathroom door. Hair — just going gray, but still more blond than ash. Breasts beginning to droop and a little belly acquired since her forty-fifth birthday last year. She sighed and shrugged into the terry cloth robe.

For dinner they ate blackberry cobbler with vanilla ice cream. When Alan came for weekends, they had regular meals. He needn't know about their sly rebellion. Grace washed the dishes, Kate dried, and they played Scrabble until bed.

Grace lay in the big old bedstead with her shade up so that moonlight could stream in the open window with the soft breeze and the buzz of katydids, the plaintive call of whippoorwills. She wanted to call Alan and share the beauty of the silvered night, but the phone worked both ways. Let him call her, if he wanted to.

Bright sunlight poured in the next morning. She had slept late; the sun was above Will's Knob. Grace swung her feet onto the cool wood floor, grabbed the cotton kimono from the nail on the closet door, and went to the bathroom. When she turned on the faucet it only hissed and gurgled, dry. She hurried downstairs to try the kitchen sink. No water, not even a rusty red trickle. Everything she counted on was drying up this year. She picked up the phone and called Alan. He answered on the first ring. So at least he was home.

"There's no water," she said.

"Is the pump working?"

"It was last night. We didn't have a storm." The prior summer the pump had been struck by lightning, burnt out, and replaced.

"Talk about a money pit. A new well."

"I wish you were here." If he were here he would take charge, calm and reassuring.

"I'm sorry, but I have a class to teach. Get drinking water in the village, use the cistern for wash water. Ask Don who he would recommend."

"Can't you come?"

"What do you think I could do you can't? Dig a well with my bare hands?"

Grace hung up. She was surprised by how angry she was, as though the dry well were his fault too, another rent torn in their life. She scooped blackberry cobbler out of the casserole, reserving the last for Kate. The phone rang, Alan calling to apologize. She let it ring and took her breakfast outside. She savored the comfort of the sweet food and sat, rocking and eating, in the porch swing. The morning mist rose in the meadow and hung tangled in the treetops. Two deer stepped out of the forest, head and shoulders breaking through the mist like cartoon animals stepping out of the page of a book. The screen door slammed and the deer bounded away.

"There's no water," Kate said.

"I know."

"What's the matter?"

"I think the well has run dry. I'm going down to the village to get water from the spring, and ask Don about the well."

"I'll come with you."

"Then have something to eat, there's cobbler. Get dressed."

They loaded the big plastic jugs into the back of the station wagon and drove down the ridge road to the village. Grace passed the two bars, the post office, and stopped in front of the general store. There, a spigot ran constantly into an old stone trough. She remembered Alan's enthusiastic explanation to the girls, "It's an artesian spring. It doesn't need a pump. The water's own internal hydrostatic pressure is pushing it up." Grace preferred to think of it as a miracle. Cool, pure veins of water rising through rock strata. Water seeking light.

Kate filled the jugs and Grace loaded them into the car. Then Grace bent to drink from the continuous, spring-fed fountain. The water tasted clean and pure as air. She dipped her fingers in the trough and pushed her hair back, then crossed the street with her daughter and climbed the steps to Don's.

Don's Hardware, a ramshackle clapboard store front with a broad porch, stretched along the one street. Don was mayor of the village, the major landholder, and ran its only successful business. Grace threaded her way through bales of barbed wire and flats of annuals on the porch. The bell above the door jangled as she walked in. Inside, it was dim and dusty. Grace inhaled. She loved the smell of hardware stores — metal and oil, paint and wood. The two-room store was packed solid with merchandise. It was like walking into a Sears catalogue, a catalogue where years and vintages mingled, new and old and in between. Neon orange hunting vests and visored caps, pressure cookers and mason jars, light bulbs and lamp oil, vise grip pliers and needle nose pliers, bins of nails, baseball gloves and badminton racquets, and bandannas in every color and pattern. In the attached garage Don sold and repaired heavy machines — washers, lawn tractors. The general store across the street struggled to get by, especially since being fined for allowing the purchase of cigarettes with food stamps. But Don's Hardware was a steady success. Don, his wife, and their sons worked as hard as their farm customers, available behind the counter from dawn to dusk, except Sundays, and on call at home even in the middle of the night in case of a plumbing or heating emergency.

"Morning, Grace, Kate," said Don's wife, almost hidden behind the high counter. The plump little woman had to stand on a stepstool to boost her high enough to operate the cash register.

"How are you, Myra?"

"Fine, thanks. How about you?"

"Okay, but we don't have water."

Don came into the store from the garage door and stood beside his wife, towering over her.

"The pump?" he asked, wiping his hands on a rag, fixing Grace with his sympathetic gaze.

"I don't think so."

"I'll send one of the boys up, to take a look. If it's not the pump, you'll have to drill. Want me to call Hiram Spurling for you, see when he could fit you in, if need be?"

"I'd appreciate it."

Don dialed.

"Don here. Looks like the folks who bought the Carr place up on the ridge need a new well drilled...Grace and Alan Murray... You know the place...Thanks." He hung up and said to Grace, "That was his wife. She said he'll come by, soon as he can. Not before tomorrow."

"Thanks. Now, I need a new ring for my pressure cooker. I want to make some apple sauce with those Early Transparents over at Sleeks Orchard."

Grace went into the back room where the shelves overflowed with cooking and canning implements — wide-mouthed glass jars, metal lids and rubber seals, candy thermometers and potato ricers. Kate was already there, sorting through the pile of bandannas; her mother let her buy one every time they came. Grace liked to make as many small purchases in the village as possible, buying light bulbs and batteries at Don's even though it would be cheaper to bring them from Pittsburgh. She shopped here partly because Alan reminded her it was important to support the local economy, but also for the pleasure of leaning on the counter to visit. Grace found her pressure cooker ring; Kate selected a bandanna emblazoned with John Deere tractors.

"You're getting so pretty, Kate," Don's wife said as she rung up their purchases.

"Thank you," said Kate, blushing. It was more than true, Grace thought. Slender, leggy Kate was just passing the threshold from pretty to beautiful.

Don's son came late that afternoon. He was skinny and tan, maybe only seventeen or eighteen, but seemed older, work hardened, shrewd in the way boys did out here. Kate looked up from reading on the porch swing. Grace saw him admire the girl, her long legs in shorts, hint of bosom beneath the tee shirt, oval face framed by blond hair. Kate smiled at him.

"Thanks for coming," Grace said, stepping between them. "Cellar door open?"

"Go on down through the kitchen. The stairs are over there."

A few minutes later he returned, "Not the pump," he said.

"Thanks for checking. And thank your father for fixing us up with Mr. Spurling."

He climbed into the dusty van, *Don's Hardware* painted on the side, and drove away, tossing a wave out the window, blowing his horn. Saluting Kate, Grace thought.

"He's kind of cute, isn't he?" she teased her daughter, trying to make light of it. She was losing Kate, too. The boy from the next farm down the road often came to take her for ice cream.

Kate shook her head and went back to her book. Grace sat with her and tried to read from the collection of poems Alan had given her last Christmas — William Carlos Williams, one of her favorites. It was hard to concentrate. The sun moved lower, swollen and gorged with the last radiance of the summer's day. She missed Alan and sitting with him to watch the sunset, sipping a glass of wine. His car pulled up, as though summoned by her reverie. She walked to the top of the porch steps. He crossed the grass, looking neat and reliable as ever, in his eternal summer uniform of khakis and plaid sport shirt.

"We didn't expect you till Saturday," she said.

"Are you disappointed?" he asked, pausing on the steps. "I thought you wanted some company, some help."

They were just two steps apart; he gazed up at her. His gray eyes, his square jaw, were so familiar she often looked but did not really see him, like casting a perfunctory glance at her own reflection. She studied him now, though. *I should kiss him,* she thought. *It would be simple, just lean down and kiss him.* But she could not.

"Did you bring the mail?"

"In my briefcase. Nothing thrilling. Hey, Kate." He crossed the porch to the girl; Grace envied the casual kiss he dropped on their daughter's hair. "What do you say to a swim before dark? You've had a hot day with no water."

He drove the back way to the lake, bouncing down the dusty, rutted dirt road between their neighbor's fields. Grace closed her eyes and imagined the cool, liquid envelope of lake water slipping over her. She almost reached across the car seat to put her hand in his lap. She looked at him; his eyes were on the road. Unease hung between them,

167

like the bulletproof shield of scratched plastic between driver and passenger in a taxicab. Last winter, in the fresh pain of discovering his betrayal, she had understood how crimes of passion happen. Some unlucky moment, the means at hand. She had needed a barrier between them at first. Now she wanted but hesitated to take it down. She had been caught off guard by his affair. If there had been warning signs, she missed them. Could she trust herself to read him now, to be sure it was over?

The lake was glass smooth, like a mirror dropped in the pocket of the hemlock forest around it. Camping families had left the beach; evening fishermen were just starting out from the boat launch. Kate ran ahead along the path past the picnic pavilions, up over the rise and down to the shore, kicking through the rough sand the park rangers trucked in each spring for a beach. Alan chased his daughter, splashing and shrieking, into the water. They ran through the shallows, then plunged and swam to the float tethered farther out. Grace waded in and stood knee deep, watching them, shading her eyes with her hand against the last slanting rays of sun.

Alan sat on the float, staring at her across the water. She sucked in her stomach and wished she had her new suit on now instead of this navy blue tank suit, stretched and baggy from too many summers. Grace waded deeper and then dog paddled out toward the float. During her childhood summers in Missouri, she had played in the stream and pond, but there had been no real swimming. She learned late, and did not like to submerge her head. "You look like a turtle, swimming with your head up," he often teased her. "What are you afraid of?" Now, she put her head under. *Stroke, stroke, breathe,* she told herself, trying not to sputter.

She reached the float and he pulled her up. It was the first time they had touched since his arrival. Kate swam around them in circles. The sun dipped behind the hemlocks as they sat on the gently rocking float.

"How about the Frosty Bear, for dinner? Save you the trouble of cooking, without water," he said. He dove off the float before she could answer and swam toward shore with Kate laughing and splashing in his wake.

Grace watched his strong, smooth stroke. She sat on the edge of the float and pushed herself in, feet first. She was glad he wasn't watching.

The Frosty Bear should have been called the Dusty Bear, sitting hard by the Route 30 entrance to the lake. Alan and Kate walked over to the window to order. Grace sat in the car and watched the local teenagers flirt, perched on the hoods of cars. Alan carried back the paper tray of burgers and fries, onion rings, milk shakes. They drove back up the ridge and ate on their own porch, cool in their damp bathing suits. Dinner finished, Kate went inside.

"Want a beer?" he asked.

"Thanks."

Their fingers touched for a moment as he handed her the smooth green bottle. She pulled her hand away. Grace listened to the drone of the katydids, watching the fireflies flicker in the meadow. The moon hung in the branches of the old walnut across the road. Alan blew soft musical notes over the mouth of his beer bottle.

"What about the spring at the bottom of the meadow?" Grace asked. They had been told cows watered there, years ago.

"Bury pipe and pump uphill? It would cost a fortune."

"I'm turning in," said Grace, irritated by his dismissive tone.

"It's early," he said, reaching up and catching her hand.

"I'm tired."

"I cancelled class, to come."

"I know, thanks," she said, going inside. She climbed the steep stairs, and wished she had stayed beside him, or that he had followed behind her and was putting his hand on her rump to play at pushing her faster up to bed.

Alone in the big oak bed, bathed in moonlight, she tried not to imagine he had stretched the cord of the phone out onto the porch, tried not to imagine he was whispering into the receiver.

She pretended to be asleep when he slid into bed beside her. Grace imagined how his shoulder would feel, if she touched him. She imagined running her fingers down the familiar planes of his face, across

169

the rough stubble of the day's growth, and then between his soft lips. *It's your move,* she told herself. *He came when you called.* But she could not reach out across the invisible line drawn down the mattress. She lay there a long time, listening to him breathe.

The next morning Grace awakened to the sound of a heavy truck groaning to a stop. Alan's side of the bed was empty. She looked out the window. A man in denim overalls walked slowly over the yard, gesturing to Alan.

Grace dressed. By the time she came downstairs, the truck was lumbering over the grass toward a wooden stake by the north side of the house. She stood guard beside the peonies. The rig was lowered into place.

The house shook all morning with the dull, constant thud of drilling. Grace and Kate escaped down the steep meadow to sit beside the moss-covered walls of the old spring but the drone carried even into the green shade of the woods. Finally it stopped and the air vibrated with quiet. Grace hurried back up the hill.

"Two hundred feet and no water. That's why they call it Dry Ridge, up here. We'll try again tomorrow. Sorry."

"Thanks for your efforts," Alan said. She could read the disappointment and frustration in his tight jaw.

The truck drove off.

"Talk about pouring money down a hole," he said. He looked defeated. For the first time in months she felt an undertow of sympathy toward him.

That evening they played badminton in the meadow across the road, Kate and Grace against Alan, batting the birdie back and forth until it grew too dark to see. Afterward, as they sat on the porch, car lights swept up the road and stopped. It was Cora, their neighbor from the dairy farm down the road. Grace and Cora had become friends over the years, going to country auctions, picking strawberries and pie cherries at the U-Pick farm in Schellsburg.

Cora stepped onto the porch. A small, gray-haired woman followed, wearing a faded flowered housedress but carrying a stick in her hand, as though on her way to a marshmallow roast.

"Evening, folks. How'd you make out?" asked Cora.

"I'm learning why they call this Dry Ridge," said Alan.

"This is Del. She could give you a hand."

"I'm a dowser. Runs in my family. Be glad to take a walk around your property, if you like."

"No need to put you out," said Alan. "They've already set up in the most likely spot for tomorrow."

"I brought a branch from a white peach. That's what works best for me."

"Never hurts to get a second opinion," said Grace.

"But it's dark," said Alan.

"There's the moon. I don't need to see to do this, so long as I don't trip."

Grace and Kate followed the two women into the yard. Alan stayed behind on the porch. The moon's silver light was so bright the women cast shadows on the grass. Del extended her arms, holding a prong of the forked branch in each hand. Del walked away from the crumpled grass where the rig had been, as though the branch were leading her. They followed. She stooped under the clothesline and passed the old stone bake oven, the outhouse, the lilac bushes. The end of the stick writhed down in the woman's outstretched hands.

"Did you see that, Mom?" Kate gasped.

Cora picked up stones and made a cairn to mark the spot.

"Want to see what it feels like?" Del asked. "Hold on with me."

Kate stood beside her.

"I'll hold one fork, you hold the other. Let's go over by the cistern."

They walked over the grass, yoked together by the branch. The stick jerked down by the cistern pump.

"Oh! Try it, Mom."

Grace took Kate's place and walked across the yard with the woman, the stick inert between them. She felt foolish, and remembered a pantomime skit of a man walking an imaginary dog. Then the rough bark scratched her palm as the branch twisted down, stirring in her hand.

"Dad, you've got to do this," Kate called up to the porch.

"I don't think so," he said.

"Come on."

He came and held the branch with Del. They walked toward the cistern. When it dipped, he let go as though it were hot to the touch.

Back on the porch, Grace lit the kerosene lantern and poured everyone a glass of cherry cordial made the summer before.

"Dowsing is a gift like any other," explained Del to Kate. "You know, like some people have perfect pitch. Keep the branch, if you like."

The women left. Kate went up to bed, holding the stick like a magic wand.

Alan and Grace sat at opposite ends of the porch swing.

"Let's ask him to move the rig," said Grace.

"Based on what evidence?"

"What have we got to lose?"

He did not reply for a long time. In the soft lamplight he looked younger, vulnerable.

"If I take this on faith, could you return the favor?" he asked, staring at her.

Grace looked away and watched the moths hovering over the lamp chimney. She swilled the last drop of sweet cordial around her mouth, and swallowed. Grace thought of artesian springs, finding a way through rock strata that seem impermeable. She took a breath as though preparing herself to swim in deep water, slid across the porch swing, and leaned on his shoulder. They rocked back and forth. The truck had bruised a corner of her garden; the night air was spiced with the sharp fragrance of crushed lavender.

About the Author

Ellen Prentiss Campbell's fiction has been featured in journals including *The American Literary Review*, *The Massachusetts Review*, and *The Southampton Review*. Her essays and reviews have appeared in *The Fiction Writers Review*, where she is a contributing editor, and in *The Washington Independent Review of Books*. A graduate of the Bennington Writing Seminars and the Simmons School of Social Work, she is a practicing psychotherapist. She lives with her husband in Washington, D.C. and Manns Choice, Pennsylvania.

Visit www.ellencampbell.net

(Photographer: Victoria Ruan)

Other Titles from The Broadkill River Press

Sounding the Atlantic
ISBN 978-0-9826030-1-7

Poetry by Martin Galvin
$14.95

That Deep & Steady Hum
ISBN 978-0-9826030-2-4

Poetry by Mary Ann Larkin
$14.95

Exile at Sarzanna
ISBN 978-0-9826030-5-5

Poetry by Laura Brylawski-Miller
$12.00

The Year of the Dog Throwers
ISBN 978-0-9826030-3-1

Poetry by Sid Gold
$12.00

Domain of the Lower Air †
ISBN 978-0-9826030-4-8

Fiction by Maryanne Khan
$14.95

Speed Enforced by Aircraft *†
ISBN 978-0-9826030-6-2

Poetry by Richard Peabody
$15.95

Dutiful Heart
ISBN 978-1-940120-91-1

Poetry by Joy Gaines-Friedler
$16.00

Necessary Myths þ
ISBN 978-1-940120-92-8

Poetry by Grant Clauser
$14.95

Other Titles from The Broadkill River Press

Postcard from Bologna ‡
ISBN 978-1-940-120-90-4

Poetry by Howard Gofreed
$15.95

Lemon Light
ISBN 978-1-940120-94-2

Poetry by H. A. Maxson
$15.95

Peregrine Nation þ
ISBN 978-1-940120-85-0

Poetry by Lucian Mattison
$15.95

On Gannon Street
ISBN 978-1-940120-86-7

Poetry by Mary Ann Larkin
$12.00

The Table of the Elements *
ISBN 978-1-940120-93-5

Poetry by J. T. Whitehead
$15.95

Good with Oranges *
ISBN 978-1-940120-83-6

Poetry by Sid Gold
$16.00

Forthcoming Titles:

Valdemar's Corpse   Delaware Literary History by Steven Leech
2015 Dogfish Head Poetry Prize Winner
The Caribbean Venture   Fiction by Edward M. Lukacs
Rock Taught   Poetry by David McAleavey
Noise   Poetry by W. M. Rivera

(* NBA Nominees) († Pulitzer Prize Nominee)
(‡ NBCC Award nominee)(þ Dogfish Head Poetry Prize Winner)

Chapbooks from The Broadkill Press

Loopholes **Poetry by David P. Kozinski**
2009 Dogfish Head Poetry Prize Winner
ISBN 978-0-9826030-0-0 $7.00

Fractured Light **Poetry by Amanda Newell**
2010 Dogfish Head Poetry Prize Winner
ISBN 978-0-9826030-7-9 $7.95

Salmagundi **Poetry by Sherry Gage Chappelle**
2011 Dogfish Head Poetry Prize Winner
ISBN 978-0-9826030-9-3 $9.00

The Softened Ground **Poetry by Tina Raye Dayton**
2012 Dogfish Head Poetry Prize Winner
ISBN 978-0-9837789-0-5 $9.00

Constructing Fiction **Essays by Jamie Brown**
ISBN 978-0-9826030-8-6 $6.00

L'Heure bleu meta-fiction by David R. Slavitt
ISBN 978-0-9837789-1-2 $11.95

The Homestead Poems **Poetry by Gary Hanna**
Honoring the 75th Anniversary of The Rehoboth Art League
ISBN 978-0-9837789-2-9 $10.95

Sakura: A Cycle of Haiku **Poetry by Jamie Brown**
ISBN 978-0-9837789-9-8 $10.95
(Winner 2013 Best Book of Verse, Delaware Press Association)

The Key Poetry Series Chapbooks from
The Broadkill Press (Series One)

The Black Narrows   Poetry by S. Scott Whitaker
     ISBN 978-0-9837789-3-6 $9.95

Ice Solstice   Poetry by Kelley Jean White
     ISBN 978-0-9837789-4-3 $8.95

Sediment and Other Poems   Poetry by Gary Hanna
     ISBN 978-0-9837789-5-0 $9.95

Sound Effects   Poetry by Nina Bennett
     ISBN 978-0-9837789-6-7 $8.95

Taken Away   Poetry by Carolyn Cecil
     ISBN 978-0-9837789-7-4 $8.95

Where Night Comes From   Poetry by Shea Garvin
     ISBN 978-0-9837789-8-1 $10.95

The Key Poetry Series Chapbooks from
The Broadkill Press (Series Two)

charmed life   Poetry by Buck Downs
    ISBN 978-1-940120-96-6 $10.95

The Stories We Tell   Poetry by Irene Fick
    ISBN 978-1-940120-98-0 $9.95
(Winner 2014 Best Book of Verse, Delaware Press Association)
(Winner , 2014 Best Book of Poetry, National Federation of Press Women)

Brackish Water   Poetry by Michael Blaine
    ISBN 978-1-940120-99-7 $10.95

Love, War and Music   Poetry by Franetta McMillian
    ISBN 978-1-940-120-89-8 $9.95

Highway 78   Poetry by Susanne Bostick Allen
    ISBN 978-1-940120-80-5 $9.95

FLUX Quanta   Poetry by James Michael Robbins
    ISBN 978-1-940120-81-2 $9.95

The Key Poetry Series Chapbooks from
The Broadkill Press (Series Three)

Silence, Interrupted   Poetry by Jim Bourey
    ISBN 978-1—940120-87-4 $9.95

Forthccoming:

Matchstick & Bramble   Poetry by Lucy Simpson
    ISBN 978-1-940120-87-4 $10.95

CPSIA information can be obtained
at www.ICGtesting.com
Printed in the USA
FFOW01n1510180116
20397FF